15 STORIES

15 STORIES

Selected by

HERBERT BARROWS
DEPARTMENT OF ENGLISH
UNIVERSITY OF MICHIGAN

D. C. HEATH AND COMPANY: 1950

CONTENTS

FOREWORD   ix

1 THOMAS HARDY
A Tradition of 1804   3

2 STEPHEN CRANE
The Open Boat   12

3 ERNEST HEMINGWAY
Now I Lay Me   42

4 DYLAN THOMAS
Patricia, Edith, and Arnold   52

5 ANTON CHEKHOV
The Schoolmistress   64

6 ANTON CHEKHOV
The Chorus Girl   75

7 WILLIAM SANSOM
How Claeys Died   82

8 NATHANIEL HAWTHORNE
Ethan Brand   96

9 JAMES JOYCE
A Painful Case   116

10 GUY DE MAUPASSANT
Happiness   127

11 KAY BOYLE
Keep Your Pity   135

12 SARAH ORNE JEWETT
A White Heron   154

13 ALUN LEWIS
The Raid   167

14 D. H. LAWRENCE
The Shadow in the Rose Garden   177

15 EUDORA WELTY
A Worn Path   193

NOTES ON THE AUTHORS   204
A READING LIST   210

ACKNOWLEDGMENTS

For permission to reprint copyright material, grateful acknowledgment is made to the following publishers, agents, and authors:

George Allen & Unwin, Ltd. For *The Raid*, by Alun Lewis, from IN THE GREEN TREE. (Acknowledgment is also made to The Macmillan Company, New York, American distributors of IN THE GREEN TREE.)

Harcourt, Brace and Company, Inc. For *A Worn Path*, from A CURTAIN OF GREEN, copyright 1941, by Eudora Welty. Reprinted by permission of Harcourt, Brace and Company, Inc.

Harper & Brothers. For *A Tradition of 1804*, from LIFE'S LITTLE IRONIES, by Thomas Hardy. Copyright 1894 by Harper & Brothers. Copyright 1922 by Harper & Brothers.

Alfred A. Knopf, Inc. For *The Open Boat*, from TWENTY STORIES by Stephen Crane, by permission of Alfred A. Knopf, Inc. Copyright 1925 by William H. Crane. Copyright 1940 by Alfred A. Knopf, Inc.

The Macmillan Company. For *The Schoolmistress*, by Anton Chekhov, from THE SCHOOLMISTRESS AND OTHER STORIES, copyright 1921 by The Macmillan Company and used with their permission. For *The Chorus Girl*, by Anton Chekhov, from THE CHORUS GIRL AND OTHER STORIES, copyright 1920 by The Macmillan Company and used with their permission.

New Directions. For *Patricia, Edith, and Arnold*, by Dylan Thomas, from A PORTRAIT OF THE ARTIST AS A YOUNG DOG, copyright 1940 by New Directions and used with their permission.

Mr. William Sansom and The Society of Authors, London. For *How Claeys Died*, from SOMETHING TERRIBLE, SOMETHING LOVELY by William Sansom. (Acknowledgment is also due to Harcourt, Brace and Company, Inc., who are shortly to publish in America the volume from which this story is taken.)

Charles Scribner's Sons. For *Now I Lay Me*, from MEN WITHOUT WOMEN by Ernest Hemingway; copyright 1926, 1927, by Charles Scribner's Sons; used by permission of the publishers.

The Viking Press, Inc. For *A Painful Case*, by James Joyce, from DUBLINERS, included in THE PORTABLE JAMES JOYCE. Copyright 1946, 1947, by The Viking Press, Inc. Reprinted by permission of The Viking Press, Inc., New York. For *A Shadow in the Rose Garden*, by D. H. Lawrence, from THE PRUSSIAN OFFICER. Reprinted by permission of The Viking Press, Inc., New York.

Ann Watkins, Inc. For *Keep Your Pity*, from THIRTY STORIES by Kay Boyle, copyright 1946, published by Simon and Schuster. Reprinted by permission of Ann Watkins, Inc.

THE SHORT STORY is perhaps the most convenient of all literary forms with which to begin the study of literature according to types. On the basis of the interest which the student can be counted on to bring to the reading of short stories, he can be introduced at the college level to work which represents a marked extension, both in quality and in kind, over the stories he has read in school or independently. By reading stories more subtle and more complex than those he has been accustomed to read, he can at least begin to establish habits of response to subtlety and complexity which will be extremely useful when he approaches other forms — the novel, poetry, the drama — either less familiar or less easily controlled.

The aim of the present volume is to assemble, in economical compass, a group of stories which will offer the student an opportunity to increase his awareness of the resources of the form, and indeed of literature itself. What seems to be essential for the student who is beginning to be a serious reader is not so much a vast collection of stories — one of each "type," one from each country, many which merely repeat approaches to which he has already mastered the response — as a group of stories which will make the most serious and significant demands upon his sensitivity and skill as a reader. Central to the plan of this collection are five stories — by Chekhov, Joyce, Lawrence, and Kay Boyle — which make precisely those demands. This is not to say that the other stories are in general any less demanding, as certainly they are not less interesting, but merely that the collection was planned around a central group of "important" and sometimes complex stories of the kinds with which the beginning reader most needs to develop his acquaintance.

Other principles were responsible for the selection of other items. The Hardy story is placed at the beginning because it seemed wise to remember that somewhere behind the short story's most elaborate developments there lurks the simple, immediate interest we all take in listening to a strange or marvelous adventure well and stirringly recounted. *The Open Boat,* whatever other features it exhibits, is a powerful narrative of the everlasting human struggle with elemental forces, it makes a strong and immediate appeal to many kinds of readers, and it poses a more intricate problem of interpretation than a hasty reading might suggest. This collection is not offered as a survey of the most important writers who have shaped and are shaping the tradition of the short story, yet there are certain figures who must obviously be represented: the more one reads of contemporary British, French, Italian, or even German fiction, for example (to say nothing of American), the more one is aware of the influence Hemingway has had even on writers whose interests and aims might at first glance appear to be wholly at variance with his.

Occasionally it is advisable to reprint stories which have already appeared in anthologies, but as far as possible each new collection should be the occasion for offering the teacher material that he has not taught before, and the advent of significant new names, like those of William Sansom and the late Alun Lewis, makes it the happiest of duties to do so.

Above all, the principle has been to make each story

chosen, whatever the special reason for including it, a *good* story of its kind, a story which will reward close reading and classroom discussion. A collection of such stories will display the wide variety of temperaments which have found expression in the form and will provide interesting contrasts in subject matter and technique. The stories have been arranged, in some instances, with an eye to bringing out the differences of interest and approach which may separate two writers who are equally good in their respective ways — it is for this reason that *A White Heron* and *Keep Your Pity* are placed side by side, and *A Painful Case* and *Happiness*. But each reader, and each teacher, will perceive other useful orders of arrangement. Critical apparatus has been omitted in the belief that to include it is to usurp a privilege which teacher and student may best exercise when left to themselves.   H. B.

15
STORIES

A TRADITION OF 1804

By Thomas Hardy

The widely discussed possibility of an invasion of England through a Channel tunnel has more than once recalled old Solomon Selby's story to my mind.

The occasion on which I numbered myself among his audience was one evening when he was sitting in the yawning chimney-corner of the inn-kitchen, with some others who had gathered there, awaiting the cessation of the rain. Withdrawing the stem of his pipe from the dental notch in which it habitually rested, he leaned back in the recess behind him and smiled into the fire. The smile was neither mirthful nor sad, not precisely humorous nor altogether thoughtful. We who knew him recognized it in a moment: it was his narrative smile. Breaking off our few desultory remarks, we drew up closer, and he thus began:

"My father, as you mid know, was a shepherd all his life, and lived out by the Cove, four miles yonder, where I was born and lived likewise, till I moved here shortly afore I wer married. The cottage that first knew me stood on the top of the down, near the sea; there was no house within a mile and a half of it; it was built o' purpose for the farm-shepherd, and had no other use. They tell me that it is now pulled down, but that you can see where it stood by the mounds of earth and a few broken bricks that are still lying

3

about. It was a bleak and dreary place in winter-time, but in summer it was well enough, though the garden never came to much, because we could not get up a good shelter for the vegetables and currant bushes, and where there is much wind they don't thrive.

"Of all them years of my growing up the ones that bide clearest in my mind were eighteen hundred and three, four, and five. This was for two reasons: I had just then grown to an age when a child's eyes and ears take in and note down everything about him, and there was more at that date to bear in mind than there ever has been since with me. It was, as I need hardly tell ye, the time after the first peace, when Bonaparte was scheming his descent upon England. He had crossed the great Alp mountains, fought in Egypt, drubbed the Turks, the Austrians, and the Proossians, and now thought he'd have a slap at us. On the other side of the Channel, scarce out of sight and hail of a man standing on our English shore, the French army of a hundred and sixty thousand men and fifteen thousand horses had been brought together from all parts, and were drilling every day. Bonaparte had been three years a-making his preparations; and to ferry these soldiers and cannon and horses across he had contrived a couple of thousand flat-bottomed boats. These boats were small things, but wonderfully built. A good few of 'em were so made as to have a little stable on board each for the two horses that were to haul the cannon carried at the stern. To get in order all these, and other things required, he had assembled there five or six thousand fellows that worked at trades — carpenters, blacksmiths, wheelwrights, saddlers, and what not. Oh, 'twas a curious time!

"Every morning neighbor Boney would muster his multitude of soldiers on the beach, draw 'em up in line, practise 'em in the manoeuvre of embarking, horses and all, till they could do it without a single hitch. My father drove a flock

of ewes up into Sussex that year, and as he went along the
drover's track over the high downs thereabout he could see
this drilling actually going on — the accoutrements of the
rank and file glittering in the sun like silver. It was thought
and always said by my uncle Job, sergeant of foot (who
used to know all about these matters), that Bonaparte meant
to cross with oars on a calm night. The grand query with us
was, Where would my gentleman land? Many of the common people thought it would be at Dover; others, who knew
how unlikely it was that any skilful general would make a
business of landing just where he was expected, said he'd
go either east into the river Thames, or west'ard to some
convenient place, most likely one of the little bays inside
the Isle of Portland, between the Beal and St. Alban's Head
— and for choice the three-quarter-round Cove, screened
from every mortal eye, that seemed made o' purpose, out by
where we lived, and which I've climmed up with two tubs
of brandy across my shoulders on scores o' dark nights in
my younger days. Some had heard that a part o' the French
fleet would sail right round Scotland, and come up the
Channel to a suitable haven. However, there was much
doubt upon the matter; and no wonder, for after-years
proved that Bonaparte himself could hardly make up his
mind upon that great and very particular point — where to
land. His uncertainty came about in this wise: that he could
get no news as to where and how our troops lay in waiting,
and that his knowledge of possible places where flat-
bottomed boats might be quietly run ashore, and the men
they brought marshalled in order, was dim to the last
degree. Being flat-bottomed, they didn't require a harbor for
unshipping their cargo of men, but a good shelving beach
away from sight, and with a fair open road towards London.
How the question posed that great Corsican tyrant (as we
used to call him), what pains he took to settle it, and, above

all, what a risk he ran on one particular night in trying to do so, were known only to one man here and there; and certainly to no maker of newspapers or printer of books, or my account o't would not have had so many heads shaken over it as it has by gentry who only believe what they see in printed lines.

"The flocks my father had charge of fed all about the downs near our house, overlooking the sea and shore each way for miles. In winter and early spring father was up a deal at nights, watching and tending the lambing. Often he'd go to bed early, and turn out at twelve or one; and, on the other hand, he'd sometimes stay up till twelve or one, and then turn in to bed. As soon as I was old enough I used to help him, mostly in the way of keeping an eye upon the ewes while he was gone home to rest. This is what I was doing in a particular month in either the year four or five — I can't certainly fix which, but it was long before I was took away from the sheep-keeping to be bound prentice to a trade. Every night at that time I was at the fold, about half a mile, or it may be a little more, from our cottage, and no living thing at all with me but the ewes and young lambs. Afeard? No; I was never afeared of being alone at these times; for I had been reared in such an out-step place that the lack o' human beings at night made me less fearful than the sight of 'em. Directly I saw a man's shape after dark in a lonely place I was frightened out of my senses.

"One day in that month we were surprised by a visit from my uncle Job, the sergeant in the Sixty-first foot, then in camp on the downs above King George's watering-place, several miles to the west yonder. Uncle Job dropped in about dusk, and went up with my father to the fold for an hour or two. Then he came home, had a drop to drink from the tub of sperrits that the smugglers kept us in for housing their liquor when they'd made a run, and for burning 'em off when there was danger. After that he stretched himself out on the settle to sleep. I went to bed: at one o'clock father came home, and waking me to go and take his place, according to custom, went to bed himself. On my way out of the house I passed Uncle Job on the settle. He opened his eyes, and upon my telling him where I was going he said it was a shame that such a youngster as I should go up there all alone; and when he had fastened up his stock and waist-belt he set off along with me, taking a drop from the sperrit-tub in a little flat bottle that stood in the corner cupboard.

"By-and-by we drew up to the fold, saw that all was right, and then, to keep ourselves warm, curled up in a heap of straw that lay inside the thatched hurdles we had set up to break the stroke of the wind when there was any. To-night, however, there was none. It was one of those very still nights when, if you stand on the high hills anywhere within two or three miles of the sea, you can hear the rise and fall of the tide along the shore, coming and going every few moments like a sort of great snore of the sleeping world. Over the lower ground there was a bit of a mist, but on the hill where we lay the air was clear, and the moon, then in her last quarter, flung a fairly good light on the grass and scattered straw.

"While we lay there Uncle Job amused me by telling me strange stories of the wars he had served in and the wounds he had got. He had already fought the French in the Low Countries, and hoped to fight 'em again. His stories lasted so long that at last I was hardly sure that I was not a soldier myself, and had seen such service as he told of. The wonders of his tales quite bewildered my mind, till I fell asleep and dreamed of battle, smoke, and flying soldiers, all of a kind with the doings he had been bringing up to me.

"How long my nap lasted I am not prepared to say. But some faint sounds over and above the rustle of the ewes in the straw, the bleat of the lambs, and the tinkle of the sheep-bell brought me to my waking senses. Uncle Job was still beside me; but he too had fallen asleep. I looked out from the straw, and saw what it was that had aroused me. Two men, in boat cloaks, cocked hats, and swords, stood by the hurdles about twenty yards off.

"I turned my ear thitherward to catch what they were saying, but though I heard every word o't, not one did I understand. They spoke in a tongue that was not ours — in French, as I afterwards found. But if I could not gain the meaning of a word, I was shrewd boy enough to find out a deal of the talkers' business. By the light o' the moon I could see that one of 'em carried a roll of paper in his hand, while every moment he spoke quick to his comrade, and pointed right and left with the other hand to spots along the shore. There was no doubt that he was explaining to the second gentleman the shapes and features of the coast. What happened soon after made this still clearer to me.

"All this time I had not waked Uncle Job, but now I began to be afeard that they might light upon us, because uncle breathed so heavily through's nose. I put my mouth to his ear and whispered, 'Uncle Job.'

" 'What is it, my boy?' he said, just as if he hadn't been asleep at all.

" 'Hush!' says I. 'Two French generals —'

" 'French?' says he.

" 'Yes,' says I. 'Come to see where to land their army!'

"I pointed 'em out; but I could say no more, for the pair were coming at that moment much nearer to where we lay. As soon as they got as near as eight or ten yards, the officer with a roll in his hand stooped down to a slanting hurdle, unfastened his roll upon it, and spread it out. Then suddenly he sprung a dark-lantern open on the paper, and showed it to be a map.

" 'What be they looking at?' I whispered to Uncle Job.

" 'A chart of the Channel,' says the sergeant (knowing about such things).

"The other French officer now stooped likewise, and over the map they had a long consultation, as they pointed here and there on the paper, and then hither and thither at places along the shore beneath us. I noticed that the manner of one officer was very respectful towards the other, who seemed much his superior, the second in rank calling him by a sort of title that I did not know the sense of. The head one, on the other hand, was quite familiar with his friend, and more than once clapped him on the shoulder.

"Uncle Job had watched as well as I, but though the map had been in the lantern-light, their faces had always been in shade. But when they rose from stooping over the chart, the light flashed upward, and fell smart upon one of 'em's features. No sooner had this happened than Uncle Job gasped, and sank down as if he'd been in a fit.

" 'What is it — what is it, Uncle Job?' said I.

" 'O good God!' says he, under the straw.

" 'What?' says I.

" 'Boney!' he groaned out.

" 'Who?' says I.

" 'Bonaparty,' he said. 'The Corsican ogre. O that I had got but my new-flinted firelock, that there man should die! But I haven't got my new-flinted firelock, and that there man must live. So lie low, as you value your life!'

"I did lie low, as you mid suppose. But I couldn't help peeping. And then I too, lad as I was, knew that it was the face of Bonaparte. Not know Boney? I should think I did know Boney. I should have known him by half the light o' that lantern. If I had seen a picture of his features once, I had seen it a hundred times. There was his bullet head, his short neck, his round yaller cheeks and chin, his gloomy face, and his great, glowing eyes. He took off his hat to blow himself a bit, and there was the forelock in the middle of his forehead, as in all the draughts of him. In moving, his cloak fell a little open, and I could see for a moment his white-fronted jacket and one of his epaulets.

"But none of this lasted long. In a minute he and his general had rolled up the map, shut the lantern, and turned to go down towards the shore.

"Then Uncle Job came to himself a bit. 'Slipped across in the night-time to see how to put his men ashore,' he said. 'The like o' that man's coolness eyes will never again see! Nephew, I must act in this, and immediate, or England's lost!'

"When they were over the brow, we crope out, and went some little way to look after them. Halfway down they were joined by two others, and six or seven minutes brought them to the shore. Then, from behind a rock, a boat came out into the weak moonlight of the Cove, and they jumped in; it put off instantly, and vanished in a few minutes between the two rocks that stand at the mouth of the Cove as we all know. We climmed back to where we had been before, and I could see, a little way out, a larger vessel, though still not very large. The little boat drew up alongside, was made fast at the stern as I suppose, for the largest sailed away, and we saw no more.

"My uncle Job told his officers as soon as he got back to camp; but what they thought of it I never heard — neither did he. Boney's army never came, and a good job for me; for the Cove below my father's house was where he meant to land, as this secret visit showed. We coast-folk should have been cut down one and all, and I should not have sat here to tell this tale."

We who listened to old Selby that night have been

familiar with his simple gravestone for these ten years past. Thanks to the incredulity of the age, his tale has been seldom repeated. But if anything short of the direct testimony of his own eyes could persuade an auditor that Bonaparte had examined these shores for himself with a view to a practicable landing-place, it would have been Solomon Selby's manner of narrating the adventure which befell him on the down.

THE OPEN BOAT

By Stephen Crane

A tale intended to be after the fact. Being the experience of four men from the sunk steamer COMMODORE.

None of them knew the color of the sky. Their eyes glanced level, and were fastened upon the waves that swept toward them. These waves were of the hue of slate, save for the tops, which were of foaming white, and all of the men knew the colors of the sea. The horizon narrowed and widened, and dipped and rose, and at all times its edge was jagged with waves that seemed thrust up in points like rocks. Many a man ought to have a bath-tub larger than the boat which here rode upon the sea. These waves were most wrongfully and barbarously abrupt and tall, and each froth-top was a problem in small-boat navigation.

The cook squatted in the bottom and looked with both eyes at the six inches of gunwale which separated him from the ocean. His sleeves were rolled over his fat forearms, and the two flaps of his unbuttoned vest dangled as he bent to bail out the boat. Often he said: "Gawd! That was a narrow clip." As he remarked it he invariably gazed eastward over the broken sea.

Reprinted from *Twenty Stories* by Stephen Crane, by permission of Alfred A. Knopf, Inc. Copyright 1925 by William H. Crane, 1940 by Alfred A. Knopf, Inc.

12

The oiler, steering with one of the two oars in the boat, sometimes raised himself suddenly to keep clear of water that swirled in over the stern. It was a thin little oar and it seemed often ready to snap.

The correspondent, pulling at the other oar, watched the waves and wondered why he was there.

The injured captain, lying in the bow, was at this time buried in that profound dejection and indifference which comes, temporarily at least, to even the bravest and most enduring when, willy nilly, the firm fails, the army loses, the ship goes down. The mind of the master of a vessel is rooted deep in the timbers of her, though he commanded for a day or a decade, and this captain had on him the stern impression of a scene in the greys of dawn of seven turned faces, and later a stump of a top-mast with a white ball on it that slashed to and fro at the waves, went low and lower, and down. Thereafter there was something strange in his voice. Although steady, it was deep with mourning, and of a quality beyond oration or tears.

"Keep 'er a little more south, Billie," said he.

" 'A little more south,' sir," said the oiler in the stern.

A seat in this boat was not unlike a seat upon a bucking broncho, and by the same token, a broncho is not much smaller. The craft pranced and reared, and plunged like an animal. As each wave came, and she rose for it, she seemed like a horse making at a fence outrageously high. The manner of her scramble over these walls of water is a mystic thing, and, moreover, at the top of them were ordinarily these problems in white water, the foam racing down from the summit of each wave, requiring a new leap, and a leap from the air. Then, after scornfully bumping a crest, she would slide, and race, and splash down a long incline, and arrive bobbing and nodding in front of the next menace.

A singular disadvantage of the sea lies in the fact that after successfully surmounting one wave you discover that there is another behind it just as important and just as nervously anxious to do something effective in the way of swamping boats. In a ten-foot dingey one can get an idea of the resources of the sea in the line of waves that is not probable to the average experience which is never at sea in a dingey. As each slatey wall of water approached, it shut all else from the view of the men in the boat, and it was not difficult to imagine that this particular wave was the final outburst of the ocean, the last effort of the grim water. There was a terrible grace in the move of the waves, and they came in silence, save for the snarling of the crests.

In the wan light, the faces of the men must have been grey. Their eyes must have glinted in strange ways as they gazed steadily astern. Viewed from a balcony, the whole thing would doubtless have been weirdly picturesque. But the men in the boat had no time to see it, and if they had had leisure there were other things to occupy their minds. The sun swung steadily up the sky, and they knew it was broad day because the color of the sea changed from slate to emerald-green, streaked with amber lights, and the foam was like tumbling snow. The process of the breaking day was unknown to them. They were aware only of this effect upon the color of the waves that rolled toward them.

In disjointed sentences the cook and the correspondent argued as to the difference between a life-saving station and a house of refuge. The cook had said: "There's a house of refuge just north of the Mosquito Inlet Light, and as soon as they see us, they'll come off in their boat and pick us up."

"As soon as who see us?" said the correspondent.

"The crew," said the cook.

"Houses of refuge don't have crews," said the correspondent. "As I understand them, they are only places where clothes and grub are stored for the benefit of shipwrecked people. They don't carry crews."

"Oh, yes, they do," said the cook.

"No, they don't," said the correspondent.

"Well, we're not there yet, anyhow," said the oiler, in the stern.

"Well," said the cook, "perhaps it's not a house of refuge that I'm thinking of as being near Mosquito Inlet Light. Perhaps it's a life-saving station."

"We're not there yet," said the oiler, in the stern.

II

As the boat bounced from the top of each wave, the wind tore through the hair of the hatless men, and as the craft plopped her stern down again the spray splashed past them. The crest of each of these waves was a hill, from the top of which the men surveyed, for a moment, a broad tumultuous expanse, shining and wind-riven. It was probably splendid. It was probably glorious, this play of the free sea, wild with lights of emerald and white and amber.

"Bully good thing it's an on-shore wind," said the cook. "If not, where would we be? Wouldn't have a show."

"That's right," said the correspondent.

The busy oiler nodded his assent.

Then the captain, in the bow, chuckled in a way that expressed humor, contempt, tragedy, all in one. "Do you think we've got much of a show now, boys?" said he.

Whereupon the three were silent, save for a trifle of hemming and hawing. To express any particular optimism at this time they felt to be childish and stupid, but they all doubtless possessed this sense of the situation in their mind. A young man thinks doggedly at such times. On the other hand, the ethics of their condition was decidedly against any open suggestion of hopelessness. So they were silent.

"Oh, well," said the captain, soothing his children, "We'll get ashore all right."

But there was that in his tone which made them think, so the oiler quoth: "Yes! If this wind holds!"

The cook was bailing: "Yes! If we don't catch hell in the surf."

Canton flannel gulls flew near and far. Sometimes they sat down on the sea, near patches of brown seaweed that rolled on the waves with a movement like carpets on a line in a gale. The birds sat comfortably in groups, and they were envied by some in the dingey, for the wrath of the sea was no more to them than it was to a covey of prairie chickens a thousand miles inland. Often they came very close and stared at the men with black bead-like eyes. At these times they were uncanny and sinister in their unblinking scrutiny, and the men hooted angrily at them, telling them to be gone. One came, and evidently decided to alight on the top of the captain's head. The bird flew parallel to the boat and did not circle, but made short sidelong jumps in the air in chicken-fashion. His black eyes were wistfully fixed upon the captain's head. "Ugly brute," said the oiler to the bird. "You look as if you were made with a jack-knife." The cook and the correspondent swore darkly at the creature. The captain naturally wished to knock it away with the end of the heavy painter; but he did not dare do it, because anything resembling an emphatic gesture would have capsized this freighted boat, and so with his open hand, the captain gently and carefully waved the gull away. After it had been discouraged from the pursuit the captain breathed easier on account of his hair, and others breathed easier because the bird struck their minds at this time as being somehow grewsome and ominous.

In the meantime the oiler and the correspondent rowed. And also they rowed.

They sat together in the same seat, and each rowed an oar. Then the oiler took both oars; then the correspondent took both oars; then the oiler; then the correspondent. They rowed and they rowed. The very ticklish part of the business was when the time came for the reclining one in the stern to take his turn at the oars. By the very last star of truth, it is easier to steal eggs from under a hen than it was to change seats in the dingey. First the man in the stern slid his hand along the thwart and moved with care, as if he were of Sèvres. Then the man in the rowing seat slid his hand along the other thwart. It was all done with the most extraordinary care. As the two sidled past each other, the whole party kept watchful eyes on the coming wave, and the captain cried: "Look out now! Steady there!"

The brown mats of seaweed that appeared from time to time were like islands, bits of earth. They were traveling, apparently, neither one way nor the other. They were, to all intents, stationary. They informed the men in the boat that it was making progress slowly toward the land.

The captain, rearing cautiously in the bow, after the dingey soared on a great swell, said that he had seen the lighthouse at Mosquito Inlet. Presently the cook remarked that he had seen it. The correspondent was at the oars then, and for some reason he too wished to look at the lighthouse, but his back was toward the far shore and the waves were important, and for some time he could not seize an opportunity to turn his head. But at last there came a wave more gentle than the others, and when at the crest of it he swiftly scoured the western horizon.

"See it?" said the captain.

"No," said the correspondent slowly, "I didn't see anything."

"Look again," said the captain. He pointed. "It's exactly in that direction."

At the top of another wave, the correspondent did as he was bid, and this time his eyes chanced on a small still thing on the edge of the swaying horizon. It was precisely like the point of a pin. It took an anxious eye to find a lighthouse so tiny.

"Think we'll make it, captain?"

"If this wind holds and the boat don't swamp, we can't do much else," said the captain.

The little boat, lifted by each towering sea, and splashed viciously by the crests, made progress that in the absence of seaweed was not apparent to those in her. She seemed just a wee thing wallowing, miraculously top-up, at the mercy of five oceans. Occasionally, a great spread of water, like white flames, swarmed into her.

"Bail her, cook," said the captain serenely.

"All right, captain," said the cheerful cook.

III

hint of theme

It would be difficult to describe the subtle brotherhood of men that was here established on the seas. No one said that it was so. No one mentioned it. But it dwelt in the boat, and each man felt it warm him. They were a captain, an oiler, a cook, and a correspondent, and they were friends, friends in a more curiously iron-bound degree than may be common. The hurt captain, lying against the water-jar in the bow, spoke always in a low voice and calmly, but he could never command a more ready and swiftly obedient crew than the motley three of the dingey. It was more than a mere recognition of what was best for the common safety. There was surely in it a quality that was personal and heart-felt. And after this devotion to the commander of the boat there was this comradeship that the correspondent, for instance, who had been taught to be cynical of men, knew even at the time was the best experience of his life. But no one said that it was so. No one mentioned it.

"I wish we had a sail," remarked the captain. "We might

try my overcoat on the end of an oar and give you two boys a chance to rest." So the cook and the correspondent held the mast and spread wide the overcoat. The oiler steered, and the little boat made good way with her new rig. Sometimes the oiler had to scull sharply to keep a sea from breaking into the boat, but otherwise sailing was a success.

Meanwhile the lighthouse had been growing slowly larger. It had now almost assumed color, and appeared like a little grey shadow on the sky. The man at the oars could not be prevented from turning his head rather often to try for a glimpse of this little grey shadow.

At last, from the top of each wave the men in the tossing boat could see land. Even as the lighthouse was an upright shadow on the sky, this land seemed but a long black shadow on the sea. It certainly was thinner than paper. "We must be about opposite New Smyrna," said the cook, who had coasted this shore often in schooners. "Captain, by the way, I believe they abandoned that life-saving station there about a year ago."

"Did they?" said the captain.

The wind slowly died away. The cook and the correspondent were not now obliged to slave in order to hold high the oar. But the waves continued their old impetuous swooping at the dingey, and the little craft, no longer under way, struggled woundily over them. The oiler or the correspondent took the oars again.

Shipwrecks are *à propos* of nothing. If men could only train for them and have them occur when the men had reached pink condition, there would be less drowning at sea. Of the four in the dingey none had slept any time worth mentioning for two days and two nights previous to embarking in the dingey, and in the excitement of clambering about the deck of a foundering ship they had also forgotten to eat heartily.

For these reasons, and for others, neither the oiler nor the correspondent was fond of rowing at this time. The correspondent wondered ingenuously how in the name of all that was sane could there be people who thought it amusing to row a boat. It was not an amusement; it was a diabolical punishment, and even a genius of mental aberrations could never conclude that it was anything but a horror to the muscles and a crime against the back. He mentioned to the boat in general how the amusement of rowing struck him, and the weary-faced oiler smiled in full sympathy. Previously to the foundering, by the way, the oiler had worked double-watch in the engine-room of the ship.

"Take her easy, now, boys," said the captain. "Don't spend yourselves. If we have to run a surf you'll need all your strength, because we'll sure have to swim for it. Take your time."

Slowly the land arose from the sea. From a black line it became a line of black and a line of white, trees and sand. Finally, the captain said that he could make out a house on the shore. "That's the house of refuge, sure," said the cook. They'll see us before long, and come out after us."

The distant lighthouse reared high. "The keeper ought to be able to make us out now, if he's looking through a glass," said the captain. "He'll notify the life-saving people."

"None of those other boats could have got ashore to give word of the wreck," said the oiler, in a low voice. "Else the lifeboat would be out hunting us."

Slowly and beautifully the land loomed out of the sea. The wind came again. It had veered from the north-east to the south-east. Finally, a new sound struck the ears of the men in the boat. It was the low thunder of the surf on the shore. "We'll never be able to make the lighthouse now," said the captain. "Swing her head a little more north, Billie," said he.

" 'A little more north,' sir," said the oiler.

Whereupon the little boat turned her nose once more down the wind, and all but the oarsman watched the shore grow. Under the influence of this expansion doubt and direful apprehension was leaving the minds of the men. The management of the boat was still most absorbing, but it could not prevent a quiet cheerfulness. In an hour, perhaps, they would be ashore.

Their backbones had become thoroughly used to balancing in the boat, and they now rode this wild colt of a dingey like circus men. The correspondent thought that he had been drenched to the skin, but happening to feel in the top pocket of his coat, he found therein eight cigars. Four of them were soaked with sea-water; four were perfectly scatheless. After a search, somebody produced three dry matches, and thereupon the four waifs rode impudently in their little boat, and with an assurance of an impending rescue shining in their eyes, puffed at the big cigars and judged well and ill of all men. Everybody took a drink of water.

IV

"Cook," remarked the captain, "there don't seem to be any signs of life about your house of refuge."

"No," replied the cook. "Funny they don't see us!"

A broad stretch of lowly coast lay before the eyes of the men. It was of dunes topped with dark vegetation. The roar of the surf was plain, and sometimes they could see the white lip of a wave as it spun up the beach. A tiny house was blocked out black upon the sky. Southward, the slim lighthouse lifted its little grey length.

Tide, wind, and waves were swinging the dingey northward. "Funny they don't see us," said the men.

The surf's roar was here dulled, but its tone was, nevertheless, thunderous and mighty. As the boat swam over the great rollers, the men sat listening to this roar. "We'll swamp sure," said everybody.

It is fair to say here that there was not a life-saving station within twenty miles in either direction, but the men did not know this fact, and in consequence they made dark and opprobrious remarks concerning the eyesight of the nation's life-savers. Four scowling men sat in the dingey and surpassed records in the invention of epithets.

"Funny they don't see us."

The lightheartedness of a former time had completely faded. To their sharpened minds it was easy to conjure pictures of all kinds of incompetency and blindness and, indeed, cowardice. There was the shore of the populous land, and it was bitter and bitter to them that from it came no sign.

"Well," said the captain, ultimately, "I suppose we'll have to make a try for ourselves. If we stay out here too long, we'll none of us have strength left to swim after the boat swamps."

And so the oiler, who was at the oars, turned the boat straight for the shore. There was a sudden tightening of muscle. There was some thinking.

"If we don't all get ashore ——" said the captain. "If we don't all get ashore, I suppose you fellows know where to send news of my finish?"

They then briefly exchanged some addresses and admonitions. As for the reflections of the men, there was a great deal of rage in them. Perchance they might be formulated thus: "If I am going to be drowned — if I am going to be drowned — if I am going to be drowned, why, in the name of the seven mad gods who rule the sea, was I allowed to come thus far and contemplate sand and trees? Was I brought here merely to have my nose dragged away as I was about to nibble the sacred cheese of life? It is preposterous. If this old ninny-woman, Fate, cannot do better than this, she should be deprived of the management of men's fortunes. She is an old hen who knows not her intention. If she has decided to drown me, why did she not do it in the beginning and save me all this trouble? The whole affair is absurd. . . . But no, she cannot mean to drown me. She dare not drown me. She cannot drown me. Not after all this work." Afterward the man might have had an impulse to shake his fist at the clouds: "Just you drown me, now, and then hear what I call you!"

The billows that came at this time were more formidable. They seemed always just about to break and roll over the little boat in a turmoil of foam. There was a preparatory and long growl in the speech of them. No mind unused to the sea would have concluded that the dingey could ascend these sheer heights in time. The shore was still afar. The oiler was a wily surfman. "Boys," he said swiftly, "she won't live three minutes more, and we're too far out to swim. Shall I take her to sea again, captain?"

"Yes! Go ahead!" said the captain.

This oiler, by a series of quick miracles, and fast and steady oarsmanship, turned the boat in the middle of the surf and took her safely to sea again.

There was a considerable silence as the boat bumped over the furrowed sea to deeper water. Then somebody in gloom spoke. "Well, anyhow, they must have seen us from the shore by now."

The gulls went in slanting flight up the wind toward the grey desolate east. A squall, marked by dingy clouds, and clouds brick-red, like smoke from a burning building, appeared from the south-east.

"What do you think of those life-saving people? Ain't they peaches?"

"Funny they haven't seen us."

"Maybe they think we're out here for sport! Maybe they think we're fishin'. Maybe they think we're damned fools."

It was a long afternoon. A changed tide tried to force them southward, but the wind and wave said northward. Far ahead, where coast-line, sea, and sky formed their mighty angle, there were little dots which seemed to indicate a city on the shore.

"St. Augustine?"

The captain shook his head. "Too near Mosquito Inlet."

And the oiler rowed, and then the correspondent rowed. Then the oiler rowed. It was a weary business. The human back can become the seat of more aches and pains than are registered in books for the composite anatomy of a regiment. It is a limited area, but it can become the theatre of innumerable muscular conflicts, tangles, wrenches, knots, and other comforts.

"Did you ever like to row, Billie?" asked the correspondent.

"No," said the oiler. "Hang it!"

When one exchanged the rowing-seat for a place in the bottom of the boat, he suffered a bodily depression that caused him to be careless of everything save an obligation to wiggle one finger. There was cold sea-water swashing to and fro in the boat, and he lay in it. His head, pillowed on a thwart, was within an inch of the swirl of a wave crest, and sometimes a particularly obstreperous sea came inboard and drenched him once more. But these matters did not annoy him. It is almost certain that if the boat had capsized he would have tumbled comfortably out upon the ocean as if he felt sure that it was a great soft mattress.

"Look! There's a man on the shore!"

"Where?"

"There! See 'im? See 'im?"

"Yes, sure! He's walking along."

"Now he's stopped. Look! He's facing us!"

"He's waving at us!"

"So he is! By thunder!"

"Ah, now we're all right! Now we're all right! There'll be a boat out here for us in half-an-hour."

"He's going on. He's running. He's going up to that house there."

The remote beach seemed lower than the sea, and it required a searching glance to discern the little black figure. The captain saw a floating stick and they rowed to it. A bath-towel was by some weird chance in the boat, and, tying this on the stick, the captain waved it. The oarsman did not dare turn his head, so he was obliged to ask questions.

"What's he doing now?"

"He's standing still again. He's looking, I think. . . . There he goes again. Toward the house. . . . Now he's stopped again."

"Is he waving at us?"

"No, not now! he was, though."

"Look! There comes another man!"

"He's running."

"Look at him go, would you."

"Why, he's on a bicycle. Now he's met the other man. They're both waving at us. Look!"

"There comes something up the beach."

"What the devil is that thing?"

"Why, it looks like a boat."

"Why, certainly it's a boat."

"No, it's on wheels."

"Yes, so it is. Well, that must be the life-boat. They drag them along shore on a wagon."

"That's the life-boat, sure."

"No, by —— , it's — it's an omnibus."

"I tell you it's a life-boat."

"It is not! It's an omnibus. I can see it plain. See? One of these big hotel omnibuses."

"By thunder, you're right. It's an omnibus, sure as fate. What do you suppose they are doing with an omnibus? Maybe they are going around collecting the life-crew, hey?"

"That's it, likely. Look! There's a fellow waving a little black flag. He's standing on the steps of the omnibus. There come those other two fellows. Now they're all talking together. Look at the fellow with the flag. Maybe he ain't waving it."

"That ain't a flag, is it? That's his coat. Why, certainly, that's his coat."

"So it is. It's his coat. He's taken it off and is waving it around his head. But would you look at him swing it."

"Oh, say, there isn't any life-saving station there. That's just a winter resort hotel omnibus that has brought over some of the boarders to see us drown."

"What's that idiot with the coat mean? What's he signaling, anyhow?"

"It looks as if he were trying to tell us to go north. There must be a life-saving station up there."

"No! He thinks we're fishing. Just giving us a merry hand. See? Ah, there, Willie!"

"Well, I wish I could make something out of those signals. What do you suppose he means?"

"He don't mean anything. He's just playing."

"Well, if he'd just signal us to try the surf again, or to go to sea and wait, or go north, or go south, or go to hell — there would be some reason in it. But look at him. He just stands there and keeps his coat revolving like a wheel. The ass!"

"There come more people."

"Now there's quite a mob. Look! Isn't that a boat?"

"Where? Oh, I see where you mean. No, that's no boat."

"That fellow is still waving his coat."

"He must think we like to see him do that. Why don't he quit it? It don't mean anything."

"I don't know. I think he is trying to make us go north. It must be that there's a life-saving station there somewhere."

"Say, he ain't tired yet. Look at 'im wave."

"Wonder how long he can keep that up. He's been revolving his coat ever since he caught sight of us. He's an idiot. Why aren't they getting men to bring a boat out? A fishing boat — one of those big yawls — could come out here all right. Why don't he do something?"

"Oh, it's all right, now."

"They'll have a boat out here for us in less than no time, now that they've seen us."

A faint yellow tone came into the sky over the low land. The shadows on the sea slowly deepened. The wind bore coldness with it, and the men began to shiver.

"Holy smoke!" said one, allowing his voice to express his impious mood, "if we keep on monkeying out here! If we've got to flounder out here all night!"

"Oh, we'll never have to stay here all night! Don't you worry. They've seen us now, and it won't be long before they'll come chasing out after us."

The shore grew dusky. The man waving a coat blended gradually into this gloom, and it swallowed in the same manner the omnibus and the group of people. The spray, when it dashed uproariously over the side, made the voyagers shrink and swear like men who were being branded.

"I'd like to catch the chump who waved the coat. I feel like soaking him one, just for luck."

"Why? What did he do?"

"Oh, nothing, but then he seemed so damned cheerful."

In the meantime the oiler rowed, and then the correspondent rowed, and then the oiler rowed. Grey-faced and

bowed forward, they mechanically, turn by turn, plied the
leaden oars. The form of the lighthouse had vanished from
the southern horizon, but finally a pale star appeared, just
lifting from the sea. The streaked saffron in the west passed
before the all-merging darkness, and the sea to the east was
black. The land had vanished, and was expressed only by
the low and drear thunder of the surf.

"If I am going to be drowned — if I am going to be
drowned — if I am going to be drowned, why, in the name
of the seven mad gods who rule the sea, was I allowed to
come thus far and contemplate sand and trees? Was I
brought here merely to have my nose dragged away as I
was about to nibble the sacred cheese of life?"

The patient captain, drooped over the water-jar, was
sometimes obliged to speak to the oarsman.

"Keep her head up! Keep her head up!"

" 'Keep her head up,' sir." The voices were weary and low.

This was surely a quiet evening. All save the oarsman
lay heavily and listlessly in the boat's bottom. As for him,
his eyes were just capable of noting the tall black waves
that swept forward in a most sinister silence, save for an
occasional subdued growl of a crest.

The cook's head was on a thwart, and he looked without
interest at the water under his nose. He was deep in other
scenes. Finally he spoke. "Billie," he murmured, dreamfully,
"what kind of pie do you like best?"

V

"Pie," said the oiler and the correspondent, agitatedly.
"Don't talk about those things, blast you!"

"Well," said the cook, "I was just thinking about ham
sandwiches, and ——"

A night on the sea in an open boat is a long night. As
darkness settled finally, the shine of the light, lifting from

the sea in the south, changed to full gold. On the northern horizon a new light appeared, a small bluish gleam on the edge of the waters. These two lights were the furniture of the world. Otherwise there was nothing but waves.

Two men huddled in the stern, and distances were so magnificent in the dingey that the rower was enabled to keep his feet partly warmed by thrusting them under his companions. Their legs indeed extended far under the rowing-seat until they touched the feet of the captain forward. Sometimes, despite the efforts of the tired oarsman, a wave came piling into the boat, an icy wave of the night, and the chilling water soaked them anew. They would twist their bodies for a moment and groan, and sleep the dead sleep once more, while the water in the boat gurgled about them as the craft rocked.

The plan of the oiler and the correspondent was for one to row until he lost the ability, and then arouse the other from his sea-water couch in the bottom of the boat.

The oiler plied the oars until his head drooped forward, and the overpowering sleep blinded him. And he rowed yet afterward. Then he touched a man in the bottom of the boat, and called his name. "Will you spell me for a little while?" he said, meekly.

"Sure, Billie," said the correspondent, awakening and dragging himself to a sitting position. They exchanged places carefully, and the oiler, cuddling down in the sea-water at the cook's side, seemed to go to sleep instantly.

The particular violence of the sea had ceased. The waves came without snarling. The obligation of the man at the oars was to keep the boat headed so that the tilt of the rollers would not capsize her, and to preserve her from filling when the crests rushed past. The black waves were silent and hard to be seen in the darkness. Often one was almost upon the boat before the oarsman was aware.

In a low voice the correspondent addressed the captain. He was not sure that the captain was awake, although this iron man seemed to be always awake. "Captain, shall I keep her making for that light north, sir?"

The same steady voice answered him. "Yes. Keep it about two points off the port bow."

The cook had tied a life-belt around himself in order to get even the warmth which this clumsy cork contrivance could donate, and he seemed almost stove-like when a rower, whose teeth invariably chattered wildly as soon as he ceased his labor, dropped down to sleep.

The correspondent, as he rowed, looked down at the two men sleeping under-foot. The cook's arm was around the oiler's shoulders, and, with their fragmentary clothing and haggard faces, they were the babes of the sea, a grotesque rendering of the old babes in the wood.

Later he must have grown stupid at his work, for suddenly there was a growling of water, and a crest came with a roar and a swash into the boat, and it was a wonder that it did not set the cook afloat in his life-belt. The cook continued to sleep, but the oiler sat up, blinking his eyes and shaking with the new cold.

"Oh, I'm awful sorry, Billie," said the correspondent contritely.

"That's all right, old boy," said the oiler, and lay down again and was asleep.

Presently it seemed that even the captain dozed, and the correspondent thought that he was the one man afloat on all the oceans. The wind had a voice as it came over the waves, and it was sadder than the end.

There was a long, loud swishing astern of the boat, and a gleaming trail of phosphorescence, like blue flame, was furrowed on the black waters. It might have been made by a monstrous knife.

Then there came a stillness, while the correspondent breathed with the open mouth and looked at the sea.

Suddenly there was another swish and another long flash of bluish light, and this time it was alongside the boat, and might almost have been reached with an oar. The correspondent saw an enormous fin speed like a shadow through the water, hurling the crystalline spray and leaving the long glowing trail.

The correspondent looked over his shoulder at the captain. His face was hidden, and he seemed to be asleep. He looked at the babes of the sea. They certainly were asleep. So, being bereft of sympathy, he leaned a little way to one side and swore softly into the sea.

But the thing did not then leave the vicinity of the boat. Ahead or astern, on one side or the other, at intervals long or short, fled the long sparkling streak, and there was to be heard the whirroo of the dark fin. The speed and power of the thing was greatly to be admired. It cut the water like a gigantic and keen projectile.

The presence of this biding thing did not affect the man with the same horror that it would if he had been a picnicker. He simply looked at the sea dully and swore in an undertone.

Nevertheless, it is true that he did not wish to be alone. He wished one of his companions to awaken by chance and keep him company with it. But the captain hung motionless over the water-jar, and the oiler and the cook in the bottom of the boat were plunged in slumber.

VI

"If I am going to be drowned — if I am going to be drowned — if I am going to be drowned, why, in the name of the seven mad gods who rule the sea, was I allowed to come thus far and contemplate sand and trees?"

During this dismal night, it may be remarked that a man would conclude that it was really the intention of the seven mad gods to drown him, despite the abominable injustice of it. For it was certainly an abominable injustice to drown a man who had worked so hard, so hard. The man felt it would be a crime most unnatural. Other people had drowned at sea since galleys swarmed with painted sails, but still ——

When it occurs to a man that nature does not regard him as important, and that she feels she would not maim the universe by disposing of him, he at first wishes to throw bricks at the temple, and he hates deeply the fact that there are no brick and no temples. Any visible expression of nature would surely be pelleted with his jeers.

Then, if there be no tangible thing to hoot he feels, per- haps, the desire to confront a personification and indulge in pleas, bowed to one knee, and with hands supplicant, saying: "Yes, but I love myself."

A high cold star on a winter's night is the word he feels that she says to him. Thereafter he knows the pathos of his situation.

The men in the dingey had not discussed these matters, but each had, no doubt, reflected upon them in silence and according to his mind. There was seldom any expression upon their faces save the general one of complete weariness. Speech was devoted to the business of the boat.

To chime the notes of his emotion, a verse mysteriously entered the correspondent's head. He had even forgotten that he had forgotten this verse, but it suddenly was in his mind.

> "A soldier of the Legion lay dying in Algiers,
>   There was a lack of woman's nursing, there was dearth of
>   woman's tears;
>   But a comrade stood beside him, and he took that comrade's
>   hand,
> And he said: 'I shall never see my own, my native land.'"

In his childhood, the correspondent had been made acquainted with the fact that a soldier of the Legion lay dying in Algiers, but he had never regarded the fact as important. Myriads of his school-fellows had informed him of the soldier's plight, but the dinning had naturally ended by making him perfectly indifferent. He had never considered it his affair that a soldier of the Legion lay dying in Algiers, nor had it appeared to him as a matter for sorrow. It was less to him than the breaking of a pencil's point.

Now, however, it quaintly came to him as a human, living thing. It was no longer merely a picture of a few throes in the breast of a poet, meanwhile drinking tea and warming his feet at the grate; it was an actuality — stern, mournful, and fine.

The correspondent plainly saw the soldier. He lay on the sand with his feet out straight and still. While his pale left hand was upon his chest in an attempt to thwart the going of his life, the blood came between his fingers. In the far Algerian distance, a city of low square forms was set against a sky that was faint with the last sunset hues. The correspondent, plying the oars and dreaming of the slow and slower movements of the lips of the soldier, was moved by a profound and perfectly impersonal comprehension. He was sorry for the soldier of the Legion who lay dying in Algiers.

The thing which had followed the boat and waited, had evidently grown bored at the delay. There was no longer to be heard the slash of the cut-water, and there was no longer the flame of the long trail. The light in the north still glimmered, but it was apparently no nearer to the boat. Sometimes the boom of the surf rang in the correspondent's ears, and he turned the craft seaward then and rowed harder. Southward, some one had evidently built a watch-fire on the beach. It was too low and too far to be seen, but it made a shimmering, roseate reflection upon the bluff back of it, and this could be discerned from the boat. The wind came stronger, and sometimes a wave suddenly raged out like a mountain-cat, and there was to be seen the sheen and sparkle of a broken crest.

The captain, in the bow, moved on his water-jar and sat erect. "Pretty long night," he observed to the correspondent. He looked at the shore. "Those life-saving people take their time."

"Did you see that shark playing around?"

"Yes, I saw him. He was a big fellow, all right."

"Wish I had known you were awake."

Later the correspondent spoke into the bottom of the boat.

"Billie!" There was a slow and gradual disentanglement. "Billie, will you spell me?"

"Sure," said the oiler.

As soon as the correspondent touched the cold comfortable sea-water in the bottom of the boat, and had huddled close to the cook's life-belt, he was deep in sleep, despite the fact that his teeth played all the popular airs. This sleep was so good to him that it was but a moment before he heard a voice call his name in a tone that demonstrated the last stages of exhaustion. "Will you spell me?"

"Sure, Billie."

The light in the north had mysteriously vanished, but the correspondent took his course from the wide-awake captain.

Later in the night they took the boat farther out to sea, and the captain directed the cook to take one oar at the stern and keep the boat facing the seas. He was to call out if he should hear the thunder of the surf. This plan enabled the oiler and the correspondent to get respite together. "We'll give those boys a chance to get into shape again," said the captain. They curled down and, after a few preliminary chatterings and trembles, slept once more the dead sleep. Neither knew they had bequeathed to the cook the company of another shark, or perhaps the same shark.

As the boat caroused on the waves, spray occasionally bumped over the side and gave them a fresh soaking, but this had no power to break their repose. The ominous slash of the wind and the water affected them as it would have affected mummies.

"Boys," said the cook, with the notes of every reluctance in his voice, "she's drifted in pretty close. I guess one of you had better take her to sea again." The correspondent, aroused, heard the crash of the toppled crests.

As he was rowing, the captain gave him some whisky-and-water, and this steadied the chills out of him. "If I ever get ashore and anybody shows me even a photograph of an oar ——"

At last there was a short conversation.

"Billie. . . . Billie, will you spell me?"

"Sure," said the oiler.

VII

When the correspondent again opened his eyes, the sea and the sky were each of the grey hue of the dawning. Later, carmine and gold was painted upon the waters. The morning appeared finally, in its splendor, with a sky of pure blue, and the sunlight flamed on the tips of the waves.

On the distant dunes were set many little black cottages, and a tall white windmill reared above them. No man, nor dog, nor bicycle appeared on the beach. The cottages might have formed a deserted village.

The voyagers scanned the shore. A conference was held in the boat. "Well," said the captain, "if no help is coming we might better try a run through the surf right away. If we stay out here much longer we will be too weak to do anything for ourselves at all." The others silently acquiesced in this reasoning. The boat was headed for the beach. The correspondent wondered if none ever ascended the tall wind-tower, and if then they never looked seaward. This tower was a giant, standing with its back to the plight of the ants. It represented in a degree, to the correspondent, the serenity of nature amid the struggles of the individual — nature in the wind, and nature in the vision of men. She did not seem cruel to him then, nor beneficent, nor treacherous, nor wise. But she was indifferent, flatly indifferent. It is, perhaps, plausible that a man in this situation, impressed with the unconcern of the universe, should see the innumerable flaws of his life, and have them taste wickedly in his mind and wish for another chance. A distinction between right and wrong seems absurdly clear to him, then, in this new ignorance of the grave-edge, and he understands that if he were given another opportunity he would mend his conduct and his words, and be better and brighter during an introduction or at a tea.

"Now, boys," said the captain, "she is going to swamp, sure. All we can do is to work her in as far as possible, and then when she swamps, pile out and scramble for the beach. Keep cool now, and don't jump until she swamps sure."

The oiler took the oars. Over his shoulders he scanned the surf. "Captain," he said, "I think I'd better bring her about, and keep her head-on to the seas and back her in."

"All right, Billie," said the captain. "Back her in." The oiler swung the boat then and, seated in the stern, the cook and the correspondent were obliged to look over their shoulders to contemplate the lonely and indifferent shore.

The monstrous in-shore rollers heaved the boat high until the men were again enabled to see the white sheets of water scudding up the slanted beach. "We won't get in very close," said the captain. Each time a man could wrest his attention from the rollers, he turned his glance toward the shore, and in the expression of the eyes during this contemplation there was a singular quality. The correspondent, observing the others, knew that they were not afraid, but the full meaning of their glances was shrouded.

As for himself, he was too tired to grapple fundamentally with the fact. He tried to coerce his mind into thinking of it, but the mind was dominated at this time by the muscles, and the muscles said they did not care. It merely occurred to him that if he should drown it would be a shame.

There were no hurried words, no pallor, no plain agitation. The men simply looked at the shore. "Now, remember to get well clear of the boat when you jump," said the captain.

Seaward the crest of a roller suddenly fell with a thunderous crash, and the long white comber came roaring down upon the boat.

"Steady now," said the captain. The men were silent. They turned their eyes from the shore to the comber and waited. The boat slid up the incline, leaped at the furious top, bounced over it, and swung down the long back of the wave. Some water had been shipped and the cook bailed it out.

But the next crest crashed also. The tumbling, boiling flood of the white water caught the boat and whirled it almost perpendicular. Water swarmed in from all sides. The correspondent had his hands on the gunwale at this time, and when the water entered at that place he swiftly withdrew his fingers, as if he objected to wetting them.

The little boat, drunken with this weight of water, reeled and snuggled deeper into the sea.

"Bail her out, cook! Bail her out," said the captain.

"All right, captain," said the cook.

"Now, boys, the next one will do for us, sure," said the oiler. "Mind to jump clear of the boat."

The third wave moved forward, huge, furious, implacable. It fairly swallowed the dingey, and almost simultaneously the men tumbled into the sea. A piece of lifebelt had lain in the bottom of the boat, and as the correspondent went overboard he held this to his chest with his left hand.

The January water was icy, and he reflected immediately that it was colder than he had expected to find it on the coast of Florida. This appeared to his dazed mind as a fact important enough to be noted at the time. The coldness of the water was sad; it was tragic. This fact was somehow so mixed and confused with his opinion of his own situation that it seemed almost a proper reason for tears. The water was cold.

When he came to the surface he was conscious of little but the noisy water. Afterward he saw his companions in the sea. The oiler was ahead in the race. He was swimming strongly and rapidly. Off to the correspondent's left, the cook's great white and corked back bulged out of the water, and in the rear the captain was hanging with his one good hand to the keel of the overturned dingey.

There is a certain immovable quality to a shore, and the correspondent wondered at it amid the confusion of the sea.

It seemed also very attractive, but the correspondent knew that it was a long journey, and he paddled leisurely. The piece of life-preserver lay under him, and sometimes he whirled down the incline of a wave as if he were on a hand-sled.

But finally he arrived at a place in the sea where travel was beset with difficulty. He did not pause swimming to inquire what manner of current had caught him, but there his progress ceased. The shore was set before him like a bit of scenery on a stage, and he looked at it and understood with his eyes each detail of it.

As the cooked passed, much farther to the left, the captain

was calling to him, "Turn over on your back, cook! Turn over on your back and use the oar."

"All right, sir." The cook turned on his back, and, paddling with an oar, went ahead as if he were a canoe.

Presently the boat also passed to the left of the correspondent with the captain clinging with one hand to the keel. He would have appeared like a man raising himself to look over a board fence, if it were not for the extraordinary gymnastics of the boat. The correspondent marvelled that the captain could still hold to it.

They passed on, nearer to shore — the oiler, the cook, the captain — and following them went the water-jar, bouncing gaily over the seas.

The correspondent remained in the grip of this strange new enemy — a current. The shore, with its white slope of sand and its green bluff, topped with little silent cottages, was spread like a picture before him. It was very near to him then, but he was impressed as one who in a gallery looks at a scene from Brittany or Holland.

He thought: "I am going to drown? Can it be possible? Can it be possible? Can it be possible?" Perhaps an individual must consider his own death to be the final phenomenon of nature.

But later a wave perhaps whirled him out of this small, deadly current, for he found suddenly that he could again make progress toward the shore. Later still, he was aware that the captain, clinging with one hand to the keel of the dingey, had his face turned away from the shore and toward him, and was calling his name. "Come to the boat! Come to the boat!"

In his struggle to reach the captain and the boat, he reflected that when one gets properly wearied, drowning must really be a comfortable arrangement, a cessation of hostilities accompanied by a large degree of relief, and he was glad of it, for the main thing in his mind for some months had been horror of the temporary agony. He did not wish to be hurt.

Presently he saw a man running along the shore. He was undressing with most remarkable speed. Coat, trousers, shirt, everything flew magically off him.

"Come to the boat," called the captain.

"All right, captain." As the correspondent paddled, he saw the captain let himself down to bottom and leave the boat. Then the correspondent performed his one little marvel of the voyage. A large wave caught him and flung him with ease and supreme speed completely over the boat and far beyond it. It struck him even then as an event in gymnastics, and a true miracle of the sea. An over-turned boat in the surf is not a plaything to a swimming man.

The correspondent arrived in water that reached only to his waist, but his condition did not enable him to stand for more than a moment. Each wave knocked him into a heap, and the under-tow pulled at him.

Then he saw the man who had been running and undressing, and undressing and running, come bounding into the water. He dragged ashore the cook, and then waded towards the captain, but the captain waved him away, and sent him to the correspondent. He was naked, naked as a tree in winter, but a halo was about his head, and he shone like a saint. He gave a strong pull, and a long drag, and a bully heave at the correspondent's hand. The correspondent, schooled in the minor formulae, said: "Thanks, old man." But suddenly the man cried: "What's that?" He pointed a swift finger. The correspondent said: "Go."

In the shallows, face downward, lay the oiler. His forehead touched sand that was periodically, between each wave, clear of the sea.

The correspondent did not know all that transpired after-

ward. When he achieved safe ground he fell, striking the
sand with each particular part of his body. It was as if he
had dropped from a roof, but the thud was grateful to him.

It seems that instantly the beach was populated with
men with blankets, clothes, and flasks, and women with
coffeepots and all the remedies sacred to their minds. The
welcome of the land to the men from the sea was warm and
generous, but a still and dripping shape was carried slowly
up the beach, and the land's welcome for it could only be
the different and sinister hospitality of the grave.

When it came night, the white waves paced to and fro
in the moonlight, and the wind brought the sound of the
great sea's voice to the men on shore, and they felt that they
could then be interpreters.

NOW I LAY ME

By Ernest Hemingway

That night we lay on the floor in the room and I listened to the silk-worms eating. The silk-worms fed in racks of mulberry leaves and all night you could hear them eating and a dropping sound in the leaves. I myself did not want to sleep because I had been living for a long time with the knowledge that if I ever shut my eyes in the dark and let myself go, my soul would go out of my body. I had been that way for a long time, ever since I had been blown up at night and felt it go out of me and go off and then come back. I tried never to think about it, but it had started to go since, in the nights, just at the moment of going off to sleep, and I could only stop it by a very great effort. So while now I am fairly sure that it would not really have gone out, yet then, that summer, I was unwilling to make the experiment.

I had different ways of occupying myself while I lay awake. I would think of a trout stream I had fished along when I was a boy and fish its whole length very carefully in my mind; fishing very carefully under all the logs, all the turns of the bank, the deep holes and the clear shallow stretches, sometimes catching trout and sometimes losing them. I would stop fishing at noon to eat my lunch; sometimes on a log over the stream; sometimes on a high bank

42

under a tree, and I always ate my lunch very slowly and
watched the stream below me while I ate. Often I ran out
of bait because I would take only ten worms with me in a
tobacco tin when I started. When I had used them all I had
to find more worms, and sometimes it was very difficult
digging in the bank of the stream where the cedar trees
kept out the sun and there was no grass but only the bare
moist earth and often I could find no worms. Always though
I found some kind of bait, but one time in the swamp I
could find no bait at all and had to cut up one of the trout
I had caught and use him for bait.

Sometimes I found insects in the swamp meadows, in the
grass or under ferns, and used them. There were beetles and
insects with legs like grass stems, and grubs in old rotten
logs; white grubs with brown pinching heads that would not
stay on the hook and emptied into nothing in the cold
water, and wood ticks under logs where sometimes I found
angle-worms that slipped into the ground as soon as the log
was raised. Once I used a salamander from under an old
log. The salamander was very small and neat and agile and
a lovely color. He had tiny feet that tried to hold on to the
hook, and after that one time I never used a salamander,
although I found them very often. Nor did I use crickets,
because of the way they acted about the hook.

Sometimes the stream ran through an open meadow, and
in the dry grass I would catch grasshoppers and use them
for bait and sometimes I would catch grasshoppers and toss
them into the stream and watch them float along swimming
on the stream and circling on the surface as the current took
them and then disappear as a trout rose. Sometimes I would
fish four or five different streams in the night; starting as
near as I could get to their source and fishing them down
stream. When I had finished too quickly and the time did
not go, I would fish the stream over again, starting where

it emptied into the lake and fishing back up stream, trying
for all the trout I had missed coming down. Some nights
too I made up streams, and some of them were very exciting,
and it was like being awake and dreaming. Some of those
streams I still remember and think that I have fished in
them, and they are confused with streams I really know.
I gave them all names and went to them on the train and
sometimes walked for miles to get to them.

But some nights I could not fish, and on those nights I
was cold-awake and said my prayers over and over and
tried to pray for all the people I had ever known. That took
up a great amount of time, for if you try to remember all the
people you have ever known, going back to the earliest
thing you remember — which was, with me, the attic of the
house where I was born and my mother and father's
wedding-cake in a tin box hanging from one of the rafters,
and, in the attic, jars of snakes and other specimens that
my father had collected as a boy and preserved in alcohol,
the alcohol sunken in the jars so the backs of some of the
snakes and specimens were exposed and had turned white
— if you thought back that far, you remembered a great
many people. If you prayed for all of them, saying a Hail
Mary and an Our Father for each one, it took a long time
and finally it would be light, and then you could go to sleep,
if you were in a place where you could sleep in the daylight.

On those nights I tried to remember everything that had
ever happened to me, starting with just before I went to
the war and remembering back from one thing to another.
I found I could only remember back to that attic in my
grandfather's house. Then I would start there and remember
this way again, until I reached the war.

I remember, after my grandfather died we moved away
from that house and to a new house designed and built by
my mother. Many things that were not to be moved were

burned in the back-yard and I remember those jars from the attic being thrown in the fire, and how they popped in the heat and the fire flamed up from the alcohol. I remember the snakes burning in the fire in the back-yard. But there were no people in that, only things. I could not remember who burned the things even, and I would go on until I came to people and then stop and pray for them.

About the new house I remember how my mother was always cleaning things out and making a good clearance. One time when my father was away on a hunting trip she made a good thorough cleaning out in the basement and burned everything that should not have been there. When my father came home and got down from his buggy and hitched the horse, the fire was still burning in the road beside the house. I went out to meet him. He handed me his shot-gun and looked at the fire. "What's this?" he asked.

"I've been cleaning out the basement, dear," my mother said from the porch. She was standing there smiling, to meet him. My father looked at the fire and kicked at something. Then he leaned over and picked something out of the ashes. "Get a rake, Nick," he said to me. I went to the basement and brought a rake and my father raked very carefully in the ashes. He raked out stone axes and stone skinning knives and tools for making arrow-heads and pieces of pottery and many arrow-heads. They had all been blackened and chipped by the fire. My father raked them all out very carefully and spread them on the grass by the road. His shotgun in its leather case and his game-bags were on the grass where he had left them when he stepped down from the buggy.

"Take the gun and the bags in the house, Nick, and bring me a paper," he said. My mother had gone inside the house. I took the shotgun, which was heavy to carry and banged against my legs, and the two game-bags and started toward

the house. "Take them one at a time," my father said. "Don't
try and carry too much at once." I put down the game-bags
and took in the shotgun and brought out a newspaper from
the pile in my father's office. My father spread all the blackened, chipped stone implements on the paper and then
wrapped them up. "The best arrow-heads went all to
pieces," he said. He walked into the house with the paper
package and I stayed outside on the grass with the two
game-bags. After a while I took them in. In remembering
that, there were only two people, so I would pray for them
both.

Some nights, though, I could not remember my prayers
even. I could only get as far as "On earth as it is in heaven"
and then have to start all over and be absolutely unable to
get past that. Then I would have to recognize that I could
not remember and give up saying my prayers that night and
try something else. So on some nights I would try to remember all the animals in the world by name and then the birds
and then fishes and then countries and cities and then kinds
of food and the names of all the streets I could remember
in Chicago, and when I could not remember anything at all
any more I would just listen. And I do not remember a night
on which you could not hear things. If I could have a light
I was not afraid to sleep, because I knew my soul would
only go out of me if it were dark. So, of course, many nights
I was where I could have a light and then I slept because
I was nearly always tired and often very sleepy. And I am
sure many times too that I slept without knowing it — but I
never slept knowing it, and on this night I listened to the
silk-worms. You can hear silk-worms eating very clearly in
the night and I lay with my eyes open and listened to them.

There was only one other person in the room and he was
awake too. I listened to him being awake, for a long time.
He could not lie as quietly as I could because, perhaps, he

had not had as much practice being awake. We were lying on blankets spread over straw and when he moved the straw was noisy, but the silk-worms were not frightened by any noise we made and ate on steadily. There were the noises of night seven kilometres behind the lines outside but they were different from the small noises inside the room in the dark. The other man in the room tried lying quietly. Then he moved again. I moved too, so he would know I was awake. He had lived ten years in Chicago. They had taken him for a soldier in nineteen fourteen when he had come back to visit his family, and they had given him me for an orderly because he spoke English. I heard him listening, so I moved again in the blankets.

"Can't you sleep, Signor Tenente?" he asked.

"No."

"I can't sleep, either."

"What's the matter?"

"I don't know. I can't sleep."

"You feel all right?"

"Sure. I feel good. I just can't sleep."

"You want to talk a while?" I asked.

"Sure. What can you talk about in this damn place."

"This place is pretty good," I said.

"Sure," he said. "It's all right."

"Tell me about out in Chicago," I said.

"Oh," he said, "I told you all that once."

"Tell me about how you got married."

"I told you that."

"Was the letter you got Monday — from her?"

"Sure. She writes me all the time. She's making good money with the place."

"You'll have a nice place when you go back."

"Sure. She runs it fine. She's making a lot of money."

"Don't you think we'll wake them up, talking?" I asked.

"No. They can't hear. Anyway, they sleep like pigs. I'm different," he said. "I'm nervous."

"Talk quiet," I said. "Want a smoke?"

We smoked skilfully in the dark.

"You don't smoke much, Signor Tenente."

"No. I've just about cut it out."

"Well," he said, "it don't do you any good and I suppose you get so you don't miss it. Did you ever hear a blind man won't smoke because he can't see the smoke come out?"

"I don't believe it."

"I think it's all bull, myself," he said. "I just heard it somewhere. You know how you hear things."

We were both quiet and I listened to the silk-worms.

"You hear those damn silk-worms?" he asked. "You can hear them chew."

"It's funny," I said.

"Say, Signor Tenente, is there something really the matter that you can't sleep? I never see you sleep. You haven't slept nights ever since I been with you."

"I don't know, John," I said. "I got in pretty bad shape along early last spring and at night it bothers me."

"Just like I am," he said. "I shouldn't have ever got in this war. I'm too nervous."

"Maybe it will get better."

"Say, Signor Tenente, what did you get in this war for, anyway?"

"I don't know, John. I wanted to, then."

"Wanted to," he said. "That's a hell of a reason."

"We oughtn't to talk out loud," I said.

"They sleep just like pigs," he said. "They can't understand the English language, anyway. They don't know a damn thing. What are you going to do when it's over and we go back to the States?"

"I'll get a job on a paper."

"In Chicago?"

"Maybe."

"Do you ever read what this fellow Brisbane writes? My wife cuts it out for me and sends it to me."

"Sure."

"Did you ever meet him?"

"No, but I've seen him."

"I'd like to meet that fellow. He's a fine writer. My wife don't read English but she takes the paper just like when I was home and she cuts out the editorials and the sport page and sends them to me."

"How are your kids?"

"They're fine. One of the girls is in the fourth grade now. You know, Signor Tenente, if I didn't have the kids I wouldn't be your orderly now. They'd have made me stay in the line all the time."

"I'm glad you've got them."

"So am I. They're fine kids but I want a boy. Three girls and no boy. That's a hell of a note."

"Why don't you try and go to sleep?"

"No, I can't sleep now. I'm wide awake now, Signor Tenente. Say, I'm worried about you not sleeping though."

"It'll be all right, John."

"Imagine a young fellow like you not to sleep."

"I'll get all right. It just takes a while."

"You got to get all right. A man can't get along that don't sleep. Do you worry about anything? You got anything on your mind?"

"No, John, I don't think so."

"You ought to get married, Signor Tenente. Then you wouldn't worry."

"I don't know."

"You ought to get married. Why don't you pick out some nice Italian girl with plenty of money? You could get any one you want. You're young and you got good decorations and you look nice. You been wounded a couple of times."

"I can't talk the language well enough."

"You talk it fine. To hell with talking the language. You don't have to talk to them. Marry them."

"I'll think about it."

"You know some girls, don't you?"

"Sure."

"Well, you marry the one with the most money. Over here, the way they're brought up, they'll all make you a good wife."

"I'll think about it."

"Don't think about it, Signor Tenente. Do it."

"All right."

"A man ought to be married. You'll never regret it. Every man ought to be married."

"All right," I said. "Let's try and sleep a while."

"All right, Signor Tenente. I'll try it again. But you remember what I said."

"I'll remember it," I said. "Now let's sleep a while, John."

"All right," he said. "I hope you sleep, Signor Tenente."

I heard him roll in his blankets on the straw and then he was very quiet and I listened to him breathing regularly. Then he started to snore. I listened to him snore for a long time and then I stopped listening to him snore and listened to the silk-worms eating. They ate steadily, making a dropping in the leaves. I had a new thing to think about and I lay in the dark with my eyes open and thought of all the girls I had ever known and what kind of wives they would make. It was a very interesting thing to think about and for a while it killed off trout-fishing and interfered with my prayers. Finally, though, I went back to trout-fishing, because I found that I could remember all the streams and there was always something new about them, while the girls, after I had thought about them a few times, blurred and I could not call them into my mind and finally they all blurred and all became rather the same and I gave up thinking about them almost altogether. But I kept on with my prayers and I prayed very often for John in the nights and his class was removed from active service before the October offensive. I was glad he was not there, because he would have been a great worry to me. He came to the hospital in Milan to see me several months after and was very disappointed that I had not yet married, and I know he would feel very badly if he knew that, so far, I have never married. He was going back to America and he was very certain about marriage and knew it would fix up everything.

PATRICIA, EDITH, AND ARNOLD

By Dylan Thomas

The small boy in his invisible engine, the Cwmdonkin Special, its wheels, polished to dazzle, crunching on the small back garden scattered with breadcrumbs for the birds and white with yesterday's snow, its smoke rising thin and pale as breath in the cold afternoon, hooted under the wash-line, kicked the dog's plate at the washhouse stop, and puffed and pistoned slower and slower while the servant girl lowered the pole, unpegged the swinging vests, showed the brown stains under her arms, and called over the wall: "Edith, Edith, come here, I want you."

Edith climbed on two tubs on the other side of the wall and called back: "I'm here, Patricia." Her head bobbed up above the broken glass.

He backed the Flying Welshman from the washhouse to the open door of the coal-hole and pulled hard on the brake that was a hammer in his pocket; assistants in uniform ran out with fuel; he spoke to a saluting fireman, and the engine shuffled off, round the barbed walls of China that kept the cats away, by the frozen rivers in the sink, in and out of the coal-hole tunnel. But he was listening carefully all the time, through the squeals and whistles, to Patricia and the next-door servant, who belonged to Mrs. Lewis, talking when they should have been working, calling his mother Mrs. T., being rude about Mrs. L.

He heard Patricia say: "Mrs. T. won't be back till six."

And Edith next door replied: "Old Mrs. L. has gone to Neath to look for Mr. Robert."

"He's on the randy again," Patricia whispered.

"Randy, sandy, bandy!" cried the boy out of the coal-hole.

"You get your face dirty, I'll kill you," Patricia said absent-mindedly.

She did not try to stop him when he climbed up the coal-heap. He stood quietly on the top, King of the Coal Castle, his head touching the roof, and listened to the worried voices of the girls. Patricia was almost in tears, Edith was sobbing and rocking on the unsteady tubs. "I'm standing on top of the coal," he said, and waited for Patricia's anger.

She said: "I don't want to see him, you go alone."

"We must, we must go together," said Edith. "I've got to know."

"I don't want to know."

"I can't stand it, Patricia, you must go with me."

"You go alone, he's waiting for you."

"Please, Patricia!"

"I'm lying on my face in the coal," said the boy.

"No, it's your day with him. I don't want to know. I just want to think he loves me."

"Oh, talk sense, Patricia, please! Will you come or no? I've got to hear what he says."

"All right then, in half an hour. I'll shout over the wall."

"You'd better come soon," the boy said, "I'm dirty as Christ knows what."

Patricia ran to the coal-hole. "The language! Come out of there at once!" she said.

The tubs began to slide and Edith vanished.

"Don't you dare use language like that again. Oh! your suit!" Patricia took him indoors.

She made him change his suit in front of her. "Otherwise there's no telling." He took off his trousers and danced around her, crying: "Look at me, Patricia!"

"You be decent," she said, "or I won't take you to the park."

"Am I going to the park, then?"

"Yes, we're all going to the park; you and me and Edith next door."

He dressed himself neatly, not to annoy her, and spat on his hands before parting his hair. She appeared not to notice his silence and neatness. Her large hands were clasped together; she stared down at the white brooch on her chest. She was a tall, thick girl with awkward hands, her fingers were like toes, her shoulders were wide as a man's.

"Am I satisfactory?" he asked.

"There's a long word," she said, and looked at him lovingly. She lifted him up and seated him on the top of the chest of drawers. "Now you're as tall as I am."

"But I'm not so old," he said.

He knew that this was an afternoon on which anything might happen; it might snow enough for sliding on a tray; uncles from America, where he had no uncles, might arrive with revolvers and St. Bernards; Ferguson's shop might catch on fire and all the piece-packets fall on the pavements; and he was not surprised when she put her black, straight-haired, heavy head on his shoulder and whispered into his collar: "Arnold, Arnold Matthews."

"There, there," he said, and rubbed her parting with his finger and winked at himself in the mirror behind her and looked down her dress at the back.

"Are you crying?"

"No."

"Yes you are, I can feel the wet."

She dried her eyes on her sleeve. "Don't you let on that I was crying."

"I'll tell everybody, I'll tell Mrs. T. and Mrs. L., I'll tell the policeman and Edith and my dad and Mr. Chapman, Patricia was crying on my shoulder like a nanny goat, she cried for two hours, she cried enough to fill a kettle. I won't really," he said.

As soon as he and Patricia and Edith set off for the park, it began to snow. Big flakes unexpectedly fell on the rocky hill, and the sky grew dark as dusk though it was only three in the afternoon. Another boy, somewhere in the allotments behind the houses, shouted as the first flakes fell. Mrs. Ocky Evans opened the top bay-window of Springmead and thrust her head and hands out, as though to catch the snow. He waited, without revolt, for Patricia to say, "Quick! hurry back, it's snowing!" and to pack him in out of the day before his feet were wet. Patricia can't have seen the snow, he thought at the top of the hill, though it was falling heavily, sweeping against her face, covering her black hat. He dared not speak, for fear of waking her, as they turned the corner into the road that led down to the park. He lagged behind to take his cap off and catch the snow in his mouth.

"Put on your cap," said Patricia, turning. "Do you want to catch your death of cold?"

She tucked his muffler inside his coat, and said to Edith: "Will he be there in the snow, do you think? He's bound to be there, isn't he? He was always there on my Wednesdays, wet or fine." The tip of her nose was red, her cheeks glowed like coals, she looked handsomer in the snow than in the summer, when her hair would lie limp on her wet forehead and a warm patch spread on her back.

"He'll be there," Edith said. "One Friday it was pelting

down and he was there. He hasn't got anywhere else to go, he's always there. Poor Arnold!" She looked white and tidy in a coat with a fur piece, and twice as small as Patricia; she stepped through the thick snow as though she were going shopping.

"Wonders will never cease," he said aloud to himself. This was Patricia letting him walk in the snow, this was striding along in a storm with two big girls. He sat down in the road. "I'm on a sledge," he said, "pull me, Patricia, pull me like an Eskimo."

"Up you get, you moochin, or I'll take you home."

He saw that she did not mean it. "Lovely Patricia, beautiful Patricia," he said, "pull me along on my bottom."

"Any more dirty words, and you know who I'll tell."

"Arnold Matthews," he said.

Patricia and Edith drew closer together.

"He notices everything," Patricia whispered.

Edith said: "I'm glad I haven't got your job."

"Oh," said Patricia, catching him by the hand and pressing it on her arm, "I wouldn't change him for the world!"

He ran down the gravel path on to the upper walk of the park. "I'm spoilt!" he shouted, "I'm spoilt! Patricia spoils me!"

Soon the park would be white all over; already the trees were blurred round the reservoir and fountain, and the training college on the gorse hill was hidden in a cloud. Patricia and Edith took the steep path down to the shelter. Following on the forbidden grass, he slid past them straight into a bare bush, but the bump and the pricks left him shouting and unhurt. The girls gossiped sadly now. They shook their coats in the deserted shelter, scattering snow on the seats, and sat down, close together still, outside the bowling-club window.

"We're only just on time," said Edith. "It's hard to be punctual in the snow."

"Can I play by here?"

Patricia nodded. "Play quietly then; don't be rough with the snow."

"Snow! snow! snow!" he said, and scooped it out of the gutter and made a small ball.

"Perhaps he's found a job," Patricia said.

"Not Arnold."

"What if he doesn't come at all?"

"He's bound to come, Patricia; don't say things like that."

"Have you brought your letters?"

"They're in my bag. How many have you got?"

"No, how many have you got, Edith?"

"I haven't counted."

"Show me one of yours," Patricia said.

He was used to their talk by this time; they were old and cuckoo, sitting in the empty shelter sobbing over nothing. Patricia was reading a letter and moving her lips.

"He told me that, too," she said, "that I was his star."

"Did he begin: 'Dear Heart'?"

"Always: 'Dear Heart.'"

Edith broke into real loud tears. With a snowball in his hand, he watched her sway on the seat and hide her face in Patricia's snowy coat.

Patricia said, patting and calming Edith, rocking her head: "I'll give him a piece of my mind when he comes!"

When who comes? He threw the snowball high into the silently driving fall. Edith's crying in the deadened park was clear and thin as a whistle, and, disowning the soft girls and standing away from them in case a stranger passed, a man with boots to his thighs, or a sneering, bigger boy from the Uplands, he piled the snow against the wire of the tennis court and thrust his hands into the snow like a baker making bread. As he delved and moulded the snow into loaves, saying under his breath, "This is the way it is done, ladies and gentlemen," Edith raised her head and said: "Patricia, promise me, don't be cross with him. Let's all be quiet and friendly."

"Writing 'Dear Heart' to us both," said Patricia angrily. "Did he ever take off your shoes and pull your toes and —"

"No, no, you mustn't, don't go on, you mustn't speak like that!" Edith put her fingers to her cheeks. "Yes, he did," she said.

"Somebody has been pulling Edith's toes," he said to himself, and ran round the other side of the shelter, chuckling. "Edith went to market," he laughed aloud, and stopped at the sight of a young man without an overcoat sitting in a corner seat and cupping his hands and blowing into them. The young man wore a white muffler and a check cap. When he saw the boy, he pulled his cap down over his eyes. His hands were pale blue and the ends of his fingers yellow.

The boy ran back to Patricia. "Patricia, there's a man!" he cried.

"Where's a man!"

"On the other side of the shelter; he hasn't got an overcoat and he's blowing in his hands like this."

Edith jumped up. "It's Arnold!"

"Arnold Matthews, Arnold Matthews, we know you're there!" Patricia called round the shelter, and, after a long minute, the young man, raising his cap and smiling, appeared at the corner and leant against a wooden pillar.

The trousers of his sleek blue suit were wide at the bottoms; the shoulders were high and hard, and sharp at the ends; his pointed patent shoes were shining; a red handkerchief stuck from his breast pocket; he had not been out in the snow.

"Fancy you two knowing each other," he said loudly, facing the red-eyed girls and the motionless, open-mouthed boy who stood at Patricia's side with his pockets full of snowballs.

Patricia tossed her head and her hat fell over one eye. As she straightened her hat, "You come and sit down here, Arnold Matthews, you've got some questions to answer!" she said in her washing-day voice.

Edith clutched at her arm: "Oh! Patricia, you promised." She picked at the edge of her handkerchief. A tear rolled down her cheek.

Arnold said softly then: "Tell the little boy to run away and play."

The boy ran round the shelter once and returned to hear Edith saying, "There's a hole in your elbow, Arnold," and to see the young man kicking the snow at his feet and staring at the names and hearts cut on the wall behind the girls' heads.

"Who did you walk out with on Wednesdays?" Patricia asked. Her clumsy hands held Edith's letter close to the sprinkled folds of her chest.

"You, Patricia."

"Who did you walk out with on Fridays?"

"With Edith, Patricia."

He said to the boy: "Here, son, can you roll a snowball as big as a football?"

"Yes, as big as two footballs."

Arnold turned back to Edith, and said: "How did you come to know Patricia Davies? You work in Brynmill."

"I just started working in Cwmdonkin," she said. "I haven't seen you since, to tell you. I was going to tell you to-day, but I found out. How could you, Arnold? Me on my afternoon off, and Patricia on Wednesdays."

The snowball had turned into a short snow man with a

lop-sided, dirty head and a face full of twigs, wearing a boy's cap and smoking a pencil.

"I didn't mean any harm," said Arnold. "I love you both."

Edith screamed. The boy jumped forward and the snow man with a broken back collapsed.

"Don't tell your lies, how can you love two of us?" Edith cried, shaking her handbag at Arnold. The bag snapped open, and a bundle of letters fell on the snow.

"Don't you dare pick up those letters," Patricia said.

Arnold had not moved. The boy was searching for his pencil in the snow man's ruins.

"You make your choice, Arnold Matthews, here and now."

"Her or me," said Edith.

Patricia turned her back to him. Edith, with her bag in her hand hanging open, stood still. The sweeping snow turned up the top page of a letter.

"You two," he said, "you go off the handle. Sit down and talk. Don't cry like that, Edith. Hundreds of men love more than one woman, you're always reading about it. Give us a chance, Edith, there's a girl."

Patricia looked at the hearts and arrows and old names. Edith saw the letters curl.

"It's you, Patricia," said Arnold.

Still Patricia stood turned away from him. Edith opened her mouth to cry, and he put a finger to his lips. He made the shape of a whisper, too soft for Patricia to hear. The boy watched him soothing and promising Edith, but she screamed again and ran out of the shelter and down the path, her handbag beating against her side.

"Patricia," he said, "turn round to me. I had to say it. It's you, Patricia."

The boy bent down over the snow man and found his pencil driven through its head. When he stood up he saw Patricia and Arnold arm in arm.

Snow dripped through his pockets, snow melted in his shoes, snow trickled down his collar into his vest. "Look at you now," said Patricia, rushing to him and holding him by the hands, "you're wringing wet."

"Only a bit of snow," said Arnold, suddenly alone in the shelter.

"A bit of snow indeed, he's cold as ice and his feet are like sponges. Come on home at once!"

The three of them climbed the path to the upper walk, and Patricia's footprints were large as a horse's in the thickening snow.

"Look, you can see our house, it's got a white roof!"

"We'll be there, ducky, soon."

"I'd rather stay out and make a snow man like Arnold Matthews."

"Hush! hush! your mother'll be waiting. You must come home."

"No she won't. She's gone on a randy with Mr. Robert. Randy, sandy, bandy!"

"You know very well she's shopping with Mrs. Partridge, you mustn't tell wicked lies."

"Well, Arnold Matthews told lies. He said he loved you better than Edith, and he whispered behind your back to her."

"I swear I didn't, Patricia, I don't love Edith at all!"

Patricia stopped walking. "You don't love Edith?"

"No, I've told you, it's you. I don't love her at all," he said. "Oh! my God, what a day! Don't you believe me? It's you, Patricia. Edith isn't anything. I just used to meet her; I'm always in the park."

"But you told her you loved her."

The boy stood bewildered between them. Why was Patricia so angry and serious? Her face was flushed and her eyes shone. Her chest moved up and down. He saw the long black hairs on her leg through a tear in her stocking. Her leg is as big as my middle, he thought. I'm cold; I want tea; I've got snow in my fly.

Arnold backed slowly down the path. "I had to tell her that or she wouldn't have gone away. I had to, Patricia. You saw what she was like. I hate her. Cross my heart!"

"Bang! bang!" cried the boy.

Patricia was smacking Arnold, tugging at his muffler, knocking him with her elbows. She pummelled him down the path, and shouted at the top of her voice: "I'll teach you to lie to Edith! You pig! you black! I'll teach you to break her heart!"

He shielded his face from her blows as he staggered back. "Patricia, Patricia, don't hit me! There's people!"

As Arnold fell, two women with umbrellas up peered through the whirling snow from behind a bush.

Patricia stood over him. "You lied to her and you'd lie to me," she said. "Get up, Arnold Matthews!"

He rose and set his muffler straight and wiped his eyes with the red handkerchief, and raised his cap and walked toward the shelter.

"And as for you," Patricia said, turning to the watching women, "you should be ashamed of yourselves! Two old women playing about in the snow."

They dodged behind the bush.

Patricia and the boy climbed, hand in hand, back to the upper walk.

"I've left my cap by the snow man," he remembered. "It's my cap with the Tottenham colours."

"Run back quickly," she said, "you can't get any wetter than you are."

He found his cap half hidden under snow. In a corner of the shelter, Arnold sat reading the letters that Edith had dropped, turning the wet pages slowly. He did not see the boy, and the boy, behind a pillar, did not interrupt him. Arnold read every letter carefully.

"You've been a long time finding your cap," Patricia said. "Did you see the young man?"

"No," he said, "he was gone." *But he wasn't. They wanted to go to him*

At home, in the warm living-room, Patricia made him change his clothes again. He held his hands in front of the fire, and soon they began to hurt.

"My hands are on fire," he told her, "and my toes, and my face."

After she had comforted him, she said: "There, that's better. The hurting's gone. You won't call the king your uncle in a minute." She was bustling about the room. "Now we've all had a good cry to-day."

THE SCHOOLMISTRESS*

By Anton Chekhov

At half-past eight they drove out of the town.
The highroad was dry, a lovely April sun was shining
warmly, but the snow was still lying in the ditches and in
the woods. Winter, dark, long, and spiteful, was hardly over;
spring had come all of a sudden. But neither the warmth
nor the languid transparent woods, warmed by the breath
of spring, nor the black flocks of birds flying over the huge
puddles that were like lakes, nor the marvelous fathomless
sky, into which it seemed one would have gone away so
joyfully, presented anything new or interesting to Marya
Vassilyevna who was sitting in the cart. For thirteen years
she had been schoolmistress, and there was no reckoning
how many times during all those years she had been to the
town for her salary; and whether it were spring as now, or
a rainy autumn evening, or winter, it was all the same to
her, and she always — invariably — longed for one thing
only, to get to the end of her journey as quickly as could be.

She felt as though she had been living in that part of the
country for ages and ages, for a hundred years, and it
seemed to her that she knew every stone, every tree on the
road from the town to her school. Her past was here, her
present was here, and she could imagine no other future

* Translated by Constance Garnett.

than the school, the road to the town and back again, and again the school and again the road. . . .

She had got out of the habit of thinking of her past before she became a schoolmistress, and had almost forgotten it. She had once had a father and mother; they had lived in Moscow in a big flat near the Red Gate, but of all that life there was left in her memory only something vague and fluid like a dream. Her father had died when she was ten years old, and her mother had died soon after. . . . She had a brother, an officer; at first they used to write to each other, then her brother had given up answering her letters, he had got out of the way of writing. Of her old belongings, all that was left was a photograph of her mother, but it had grown dim from the dampness of the school, and now nothing could be seen but the hair and the eyebrows.

When they had driven a couple of miles, old Semyon, who was driving, turned round and said:

"They have caught a government clerk in the town. They have taken him away. The story is that with some Germans he killed Alexeyev, the Mayor, in Moscow."

"Who told you that?"

"They were reading it in the paper, in Ivan Ionov's tavern."

And again they were silent for a long time. Marya Vassil-yevna thought of her school, of the examination that was coming soon, and of the girl and four boys she was sending up for it. And just as she was thinking about the examina-tion, she was overtaken by a neighboring landowner called Hanov in a carriage with four horses, the very man who had been examiner in her school the year before. When he came up to her he recognized her and bowed.

"Good-morning," he said to her. "You are driving home, I suppose."

This Hanov, a man of forty with a listless expression and

a face that showed signs of wear, was beginning to look old, but was still handsome and admired by women. He lived in his big homestead alone, and was not in the service; and people used to say of him that he did nothing at home but walk up and down the room whistling, or play chess with his old footman. People said, too, that he drank heavily. And indeed at the examination the year before the very papers he brought with him smelt of wine and scent. He had been dressed all in new clothes on that occasion, and Marya Vassilyevna thought him very attractive, and all the while she sat beside him she had felt embarrassed. She was accustomed to see frigid and sensible examiners at the school, while this one did not remember a single prayer, or know what to ask questions about, and was exceedingly courteous and delicate, giving nothing but the highest marks.

"I am going to visit Bakvist," he went on, addressing Marya Vassilyevna, "but I am told he is not at home."

They turned off the highroad into a by-road to the village, Hanov leading the way and Semyon following. The four horses moved at a walking pace, with effort dragging the heavy carriage through the mud. Semyon tacked from side to side, keeping to the edge of the road, at one time through a snow-drift, at another through a pool, often jumping out of the cart and helping the horse. Marya Vassilyevna was still thinking about the school, wondering whether the arithmetic questions at the examination would be difficult or easy. And she felt annoyed with the Zemstvo board at which she had found no one the day before. How unbusiness-like! Here she had been asking them for the last two years to dismiss the watchman, who did nothing, was rude to her, and hit the schoolboys; but no one paid any attention. It was hard to find the president at the office, and when one did find him he would say with tears in his eyes that he hadn't a moment to spare; the inspector visited the school at most once in three years, and knew nothing whatever about his work, as he had been in the Excise Duties Department, and had received the post of school inspector through influence. The School Council met very rarely, and there was no knowing where it met; the school guardian was an almost illiterate peasant, the head of a tanning business, unintelligent, rude, and a great friend of the watchman's — and goodness knows to whom she could appeal with complaints or inquiries. . . .

"He really is handsome," she thought, glancing at Hanov.

The road grew worse and worse. . . . They drove into the wood. Here there was no room to turn around, the wheels sank deeply in, water splashed and gurgled through them, and sharp twigs struck them in the face.

"What a road!" said Hanov, and he laughed.

The schoolmistress looked at him and could not understand why this queer man lived here. What could his money, his interesting appearance, his refined bearing do for him here, in this mud, in this God-forsaken, dreary place? He got no special advantages out of life, and here, like Semyon, was driving at a jog-trot on an appalling road and enduring the same discomforts. Why live here if one could live in Petersburg or abroad? And one would have thought it would be nothing for a rich man like him to make a good road instead of this bad one, to avoid enduring this misery and seeing the despair on the faces of his coachman and Semyon; but he only laughed, and apparently did not mind, and wanted no better life. He was kind, soft, naïve, and he did not understand this coarse life, just as at the examination he did not know the prayers. He subscribed nothing to the schools but globes, and genuinely regarded himself as a useful person and a prominent worker in the cause of popular education. And what use were his globes here?

"Hold on, Vassilyevna!" said Semyon.

The cart lurched violently and was on the point of up-
setting; something heavy rolled on to Marya Vassilyevna's
feet — it was her parcel of purchases. There was a steep
ascent uphill through the clay; here in the winding ditches
rivulets were gurgling. The water seemed to have gnawed
away the road; and how could one get along here! The
horses breathed hard. Hanov got out of his carriage and
walked at the side of the road in his long overcoat. He was
hot.

"What a road!" he said, and laughed again. "It would soon
smash up one's carriage."

"Nobody obliges you to drive about in such weather,"
said Semyon surlily. "You should stay at home."

"I am dull at home, grandfather. I don't like staying at
home."

Beside old Semyon he looked graceful and vigorous, but
yet in his walk there was something just perceptible which
betrayed in him a being already touched by decay, weak,
and on the road to ruin. And all at once there was a whiff
of spirits in the wood. Marya Vassilyevna was filled with
dread and pity for this man going to his ruin for no visible
cause or reason, and it came into her mind that if she had
been his wife or sister she would have devoted her whole
life to saving him from ruin. His wife! Life was so ordered
that here he was living in his great house alone, and she
was living in a God-forsaken village alone, and yet for some
reason the mere thought that he and she might be close to
one another and equals seemed impossible and absurd. In
reality, life was arranged and human relations were compli-
cated so utterly beyond all understanding that when one
thought about it one felt uncanny and one's heart sank.

"And it is beyond all understanding," she thought, "why
God gives beauty, this graciousness, and sad, sweet eyes to
weak, unlucky, useless people — why they are so charming."

"Here we must turn off to the right," said Hanov, getting into his carriage. "Good-by! I wish you all things good!"

And again she thought of her pupils, of the examination, of the watchman, of the School Council; and when the wind brought the sound of the retreating carriage these thoughts were mingled with others. She longed to think of beautiful eyes, of love, of the happiness which would never be. . . .

His wife? It was cold in the morning, there was no one to heat the stove, the watchman disappeared; the children came in as soon as it was light, bringing in snow and mud and making a noise: it was all so inconvenient, so comfortless. Her abode consisted of one little room and the kitchen close by. Her head ached every day after her work, and after dinner she had heart-burn. She had to collect money from the school-children for wood and for the watchman, and to give it to the school guardian, and then to entreat him — that overfed, insolent peasant — for God's sake to send her wood. And at night she dreamed of examinations, peasants, snow-drifts. And this life was making her grow old and coarse, making her ugly, angular, and awkward, as though she were made of lead. She was always afraid, and she would get up from her seat and not venture to sit down in the presence of a member of the Zemstvo or the school guardian. And she used formal, deferential expressions when she spoke of any one of them. And no one thought her attractive, and life was passing drearily, without affection, without friendly sympathy, without interesting acquaintances. How awful it would have been in her position if she had fallen in love!

"Hold on, Vassilyevna!"

Again a sharp ascent uphill. . . .

She had become a schoolmistress from necessity, without feeling any vocation for it; and she had never thought of a vocation, of serving the cause of enlightenment; and it always seemed to her that what was most important in her work was not the children, nor enlightenment, but the examinations. And what time had she for thinking of vocation, of serving the cause of enlightenment? Teachers, badly paid doctors, and their assistants, with their terribly hard work, have not even the comfort of thinking that they are serving an idea or the people, as their heads are always stuffed with thoughts of their daily bread, of wood for the fire, of bad roads, of illnesses. It is a hard-working, an uninteresting life, and only silent, patient cart-horses like Marya Vassilyevna could put up with it for long; the lively, nervous, impressionable people who talked about a vocation and serving the idea were soon weary of it and gave up the work.

Semyon kept picking out the driest and shortest way, first by a meadow, then by the backs of the village huts; but in one place the peasants would not let them pass, in another it was the priest's land and they could not cross it, in another Ivan Ionov had bought a plot from the landowner and had dug a ditch round it. They kept having to turn back.

They reached Nizhneye Gorodistche. Near the tavern on the dung-strewn earth, where the snow was still lying, there stood wagons that had brought great bottles of crude sulphuric acid. There were a great many people in the tavern, all drivers, and there was a smell of vodka, tobacco, and sheepskins. There was a loud noise of conversation and the banging of the swing-door. Through the wall, without ceasing for a moment, came the sound of a concertina being played in the shop. Marya Vassilyevna sat down and drank some tea, while at the next table peasants were drinking vodka and beer, perspiring from the tea they had just swallowed and the stifling fumes of the tavern.

"I say, Kuzma!" voices kept shouting in confusion. "What there!" "The Lord bless us!" "Ivan Dementyitch, I can tell you that!" "Look out, old man!"

A little pock-marked man with a black beard, who was

quite drunk, was suddenly surprised by something and began using bad language.

"What are you swearing at, you there?" Semyon, who was sitting some way off, responded angrily. "Don't you see the young lady?"

"The young lady!" someone mimicked in another corner. "Swinish crow!"

"We meant nothing . . ." said the little man in confusion. "I beg your pardon. We pay with our money and the young lady with hers. Good-morning!"

"Good-morning," answered the schoolmistress.

"And we thank you most feelingly."

Marya Vassilyevna drank her tea with satisfaction, and she, too, began turning red like the peasants, and fell to thinking again about firewood, about the watchman. . . .

"Stay, old man," she heard from the next table, "it's the schoolmistress from Vyazovye. . . . We know her; she's a good young lady."

"She's all right!"

The swing-door was continually banging, some coming in, others going out. Marya Vassilyevna sat on, thinking all the time of the same things, while the concertina went on playing and playing. The patches of sunshine had been on the floor, then they passed to the counter, to the wall, and disappeared altogether; so by the sun it was past midday. The peasants at the next table were getting ready to go. The little man, somewhat unsteadily, went up to Marya Vassilyevna and held out his hand to her; following his example, the others shook hands, too, at parting, and went out one after another, and the swing-door squeaked and slammed nine times.

"Vassilyevna, get ready," Semyon called to her.

They set off. And again they went at a walking pace.

"A little while back they were building a school here in

their Nizhneye Gorodistche," said Semyon, turning around. "It was a wicked thing that was done!"

"Why, what?"

"They say the president put a thousand in his pocket, and the school guardian another thousand in his, and the teacher five hundred."

"The whole school only cost a thousand. It's wrong to slander people, grandfather. That's all nonsense."

"I don't know, . . . I only tell you what folks say."

But it was clear that Semyon did not believe the schoolmistress. The peasants did not believe her. They always thought she received too large a salary, twenty one roubles a month (five would have been enough), and that of the money that she collected from the children for the firewood and the watchman the greater part she kept for herself. The guardian thought the same as the peasants, and he himself made a profit off the firewood and received payments from the peasants for being a guardian — without the knowledge of the authorities.

The forest, thank God! was behind them, and now it would be flat, open ground all the way to Vyazovye, and there was not far to go now. They had to cross the river and then the railway line, and then Vyazovye was in sight.

"Where are you driving?" Marya Vassilyevna asked Semyon. "Take the road to the right to the bridge."

"Why, we can go this way as well. It's not deep enough to matter."

"Mind you don't drown the horse."

"What?"

"Look, Hanov is driving to the bridge," said Marya Vassilyevna, seeing the four horses far away to the right. "It is he, I think."

"It is. So he didn't find Bakvist at home. What a pigheaded fellow he is. Lord have mercy upon us! He's driven over there, and what for? It's fully two miles nearer this way."

They reached the river. In the summer it was a little stream easily crossed by wading. It usually dried up in August, but now, after the spring floods, it was a river forty feet in breadth, rapid, muddy, and cold; on the bank and right up to the water there were fresh tracks of wheels, so it had been crossed here.

"Go on!" shouted Semyon angrily and anxiously, tugging violently at the reins and jerking his elbows as a bird does its wings. "Go on!"

The horse went on into the water up to his belly and stopped, but at once went on again with an effort, and Marya Vassilyevna was aware of a keen chilliness in her feet.

"Go on!" she, too, shouted, getting up. "Go on!"

They got out on the bank.

"Nice mess it is, Lord have mercy upon us!" muttered Semyon, setting straight the harness. "It's a perfect plague with this Zemstvo. . . ."

Her shoes and goloshes were full of water, the lower part of her dress and of her coat and one sleeve were wet and dripping: the sugar and flour had got wet, and that was worst of all, and Marya Vassilyevna could only clasp her hands in despair and say:

"Oh, Semyon, Semyon! How tiresome you are, really! . . ."

The barrier was down at the railway crossing. A train was coming out of the station. Marya Vassilyevna stood at the crossing waiting till it should pass, and shivering all over with cold. Vyazovye was in sight now, and the school with the green roof, and the church with its crosses flashing in the evening sun: and the station windows flashed too, and a pink smoke rose from the engine . . . and it seemed to her that everything was trembling with cold.

Here was the train; the windows reflected the gleaming

light like the crosses on the church: it made her eyes ache
to look at them. On the little platform between two first-class
carriages a lady was standing, and Marya Vassilyevna
glanced at her as she passed. Her mother! What a resem-
blance! Her mother had had just such luxuriant hair, just
such a brow and bend of the head. And with amazing dis-
tinctness, for the first time in those thirteen years, there rose
before her mind a vivid picture of her mother, her father,
her brother, their flat in Moscow, the aquarium with little
fish, everything to the tiniest detail; she heard the sound of
the piano, her father's voice; she felt as she had been then,
young, good-looking, well-dressed, in a bright warm room
among her own people. A feeling of joy and happiness suddenly came over her, she pressed her hands to her temples
in an ecstasy, and called softly, beseechingly:

"Mother!"

And she began crying, she did not know why. Just at that
instant Hanov drove up with his team of four horses, and
seeing him she imagined happiness such as she had never
had, and smiled and nodded to him as an equal and a friend,
and it seemed to her that her happiness, her triumph, was
glowing in the sky and on all sides, in the windows and on
the trees. Her father and mother had never died, she had
never been a schoolmistress, it was a long, tedious, strange
dream, and now she had awakened. . . .

"Vassilyevna, get in!"

And at once it all vanished. The barrier was slowly raised.
Marya Vassilyevna, shivering and numb with cold, got into
the cart. The carriage with the four horses crossed the railway line; Semyon followed it. The signalman took off his
cap.

"And here is Vyazovye. Here we are."

THE CHORUS GIRL*

By Anton Chekhov

One day when she was younger and better-looking, and when her voice was stronger, Nikolay Petrovitch Kolpakov, her adorer, was sitting in the outer room in her summer villa. It was intolerably hot and stifling. Kolpakov, who had just dined and drunk a whole bottle of inferior port, felt ill-humoured and out of sorts. Both were bored and waiting for the heat of the day to be over in order to go for a walk.

All at once there was a sudden ring at the door. Kolpakov, who was sitting with his coat off, in his slippers, jumped up and looked inquiringly at Pasha.

"It must be the postman or one of the girls," said the singer.

Kolpakov did not mind being found by the postman or Pasha's lady friends, but by way of precaution gathered up his clothes and went into the next room, while Pasha ran to open the door. To her great surprise in the doorway stood, not the postman and not a girl friend, but an unknown woman, young and beautiful, who was dressed like a lady, and from all outward signs was one.

The stranger was pale and was breathing heavily as though she had been running up a steep flight of stairs.

* Translated by Constance Garnett.

"What is it?" asked Pasha.

The lady did not at once answer. She took a step forward, slowly looked about the room, and sat down in a way that suggested that from fatigue, or perhaps illness, she could not stand; then for a long time her pale lips quivered as she tried in vain to speak.

"Is my husband here?" she asked at last, raising to Pasha her big eyes with their red tear-stained lids.

"Husband?" whispered Pasha, and was suddenly so frightened that her hands and feet turned cold. "What husband?" she repeated, beginning to tremble.

"My husband, . . . Nikolay Petrovitch Kolpakov."

"N . . . no, madam. . . . I . . . I don't know any husband."

A minute passed in silence. The stranger several times passed her handkerchief over her pale lips and held her breath to stop her inward trembling, while Pasha stood before her motionless, like a post, and looked at her with astonishment and terror.

"So you say he is not here?" the lady asked, this time speaking with a firm voice and smiling oddly.

"I . . . I don't know who it is you are asking about."

"You are horrid, mean, vile . . ." the stranger muttered, scanning Pasha with hatred and repulsion. "Yes, yes . . . you are horrid. I am very, very glad that at last I can tell you so!"

Pasha felt that on this lady in black with the angry eyes and white slender fingers she produced the impression of something horrid and unseemly, and she felt ashamed of her chubby red cheeks, the pock-mark on her nose, and the fringe on her forehead, which never could be combed back. And it seemed to her that if she had been thin, and had had no powder on her face and no fringe on her forehead, then she could have disguised the fact that she was not "respectable," and she would not have felt so frightened and ashamed to stand facing this unknown, mysterious lady.

"Where is my husband?" the lady went on. "Though I
don't care whether he is here or not, but I ought to tell you
that the money has been missed, and they are looking for
Nikolay Petrovitch. . . . They mean to arrest him. That's your
doing!"

The lady got up and walked about the room in great
excitement. Pasha looked at her and was so frightened that
she could not understand.

"He'll be found and arrested to-day," said the lady, and
she gave a sob, and in that sound could be heard her resent-
ment and vexation. "I know who has brought him to this
awful position! Low, horrid creature! Loathsome, mercenary
hussy!" The lady's lips worked and her nose wrinkled up
with disgust. "I am helpless, do you hear, you low woman?
. . . I am helpless; you are stronger than I am, but there is
One to defend me and my children! God sees all! He is
just! He will punish you for every tear I have shed, for all
my sleepless nights! The time will come; you will think of
me! . . ."

Silence followed again. The lady walked about the room
and wrung her hands, while Pasha still gazed blankly at her
in amazement, not understanding and expecting something
terrible.

"I know nothing about it, madam," she said, and suddenly
burst into tears.

"You are lying!" cried the lady, and her eyes flashed
angrily at her. "I know all about it! I've known you a long
time. I know that for the last month he has been spending
every day with you!"

"Yes. What then? What of it? I have a great many visitors,
but I don't force anyone to come. He is free to do as he likes."

"I tell you they have discovered that money is missing!
He has embezzled money at the office! For the sake of such
a . . . creature as you, for your sake he has actually com-

mitted a crime. Listen," said the lady in a resolute voice, stopping short, facing Pasha. "You can have no principles; you live simply to do harm — that's your object; but one can't imagine you have fallen so low that you have no trace of human feeling left! He has a wife, children. . . . If he is condemned and sent into exile we shall starve, the children and I. . . . Understand that! And yet there is a chance of saving him and us from destitution and disgrace. If I take them nine hundred roubles to-day they will let him alone. Only nine hundred roubles!"

"What nine hundred roubles?" Pasha asked softly. "I . . . I don't know. . . . I haven't taken it."

"I am not asking you for nine hundred roubles. . . . You have no money, and I don't want your money. I ask you for something else. . . . Men usually give expensive things to women like you. Only give me back the things my husband has given you!"

"Madam, he has never made me a present of anything!" Pasha wailed, beginning to understand.

"Where is the money? He has squandered his own and mine and other people's. . . . What has become of it all? Listen, I beg you! I was carried away by indignation and said a lot of nasty things to you, but I apologize. You must hate me, I know, but if you are capable of sympathy, put yourself in my position! I implore you to give me back the things!"

"H'm!" said Pasha, and she shrugged her shoulders. "I would with pleasure, but, God is my witness, he never made me a present of anything. Believe me, on my conscience. However, you are right, though," said the singer in confusion, "he did bring me two little things. Certainly I will give them back, if you wish it."

Pasha pulled out one of the drawers in the toilet-table and took out of it a hollow gold bracelet and a thin ring with a ruby in it.

"Here, madam!" she said, handing the visitor these articles.

The lady flushed and her face quivered. She was offended.

"What are you giving me?" she said. "I am not asking for charity, but for what does not belong to you . . . what you have taken advantage of your position to squeeze out of my husband . . . that weak, unhappy man. . . . On Thursday, when I saw you with my husband at the harbour you were wearing expensive brooches and bracelets. So it's no use your playing the innocent lamb to me! I ask you for the last time: will you give me the things, or not?"

"You are a queer one, upon my word," said Pasha, beginning to feel offended. "I assure you that, except the bracelet and this little ring, I've never seen a thing from your Nikolay Petrovitch. He brings me nothing but sweet cakes."

"Sweet cakes!" laughed the stranger. "At home the children have nothing to eat, and here you have sweet cakes. You absolutely refuse to restore the presents?"

Receiving no answer, the lady sat down and stared into space, pondering.

"What's to be done now?" she said. "If I don't get nine hundred roubles, he is ruined, and the children and I are ruined, too. Shall I kill this low woman or go down on my knees to her?"

The lady pressed her handkerchief to her face and broke into sobs.

"I beg you!" Pasha heard through the stranger's sobs. "You see you have plundered and ruined my husband. Save him. . . . You have no feeling for him, but the children . . . the children. . . . What have the children done?"

Pasha imagined little children standing in the street, crying with hunger, and she, too, sobbed.

"What can I do, madam?" she said. "You say that I am a low woman and that I have ruined Nikolay Petrovitch, and I assure you . . . before God Almighty, I have had nothing

from him whatever. . . . There is only one girl in our chorus
who has a rich admirer; all the rest of us live from hand to
mouth on bread and kvass. Nikolay Petrovitch is a highly
educated, refined gentleman, so I've made him welcome.
We are bound to make gentlemen welcome."

"I ask you for the things! Give me the things! I am crying.
. . . I am humiliating myself. . . . If you like I will go down
on my knees! If you wish it!"

Pasha shrieked with horror and waved her hands. She
felt that this pale, beautiful lady who expressed herself so
grandly, as though she were on the stage, really might go
down on her knees to her, simply from pride, from grandeur,
to exalt herself and humiliate the chorus girl.

"Very well, I will give you things!" said Pasha, wiping
her eyes and bustling about. "By all means. Only they are
not from Nikolay Petrovitch. . . . I got these from other
gentlemen. As you please. . . ."

Pasha pulled out the upper drawer of the chest, took out
a diamond brooch, a coral necklace, some rings and bracelets, and gave them all to the lady.

"Take them if you like, only I've never had anything
from your husband. Take them and grow rich," Pasha went
on, offended at the threat to go down on her knees. "And if
you are a lady . . . his lawful wife, you should keep him to
yourself. I should think so! I did not ask him to come; he
came of himself."

Through her tears the lady scrutinized the articles given
her and said:

"This isn't everything. . . . There won't be five hundred
roubles' worth here."

Pasha impulsively flung out of the chest a gold watch, a
cigar-case and studs, and said, flinging up her hands:

"I've nothing else left. . . . You can search!"

The visitor gave a sigh, with trembling hands twisted the

things up in her handkerchief, and went out without uttering a word, without even nodding her head.

The door from the next room opened and Kolpakov walked in. He was pale and kept shaking his head nervously, as though he had swallowed something very bitter; tears were glistening in his eyes.

"What presents did you make me?" Pasha asked, pouncing upon him. "When did you, allow me to ask you?"

"Presents . . . that's no matter!" said Kolpakov, and he tossed his head. "My God! She cried before you, she humbled herself. . . ."

"I am asking you, what presents did you make me?" Pasha cried.

"My God! She, a lady, so proud, so pure. . . . She was ready to go down on her knees to . . . to this wench! And I've brought her to this! I've allowed it!"

He clutched his head in his hands and moaned.

"No, I shall never forgive myself for this! I shall never forgive myself! Get away from me . . . you low creature!" he cried with repulsion, backing away from Pasha, and thrusting her off with trembling hands. "She would have gone down on her knees, and . . . and to you! Oh, my God!"

He rapidly dressed, and pushing Pasha aside contemptuously, made for the door and went out.

Pasha lay down and began wailing aloud. She was already regretting her things which she had given away so impulsively, and her feelings were hurt. She remembered how three years ago a merchant had beaten her for no sort of reason, and she wailed more loudly than ever.

HOW CLAEYS DIED

By William Sansom

In Germany, two months after the capitulation, tall green grass and corn had grown up round every remnant of battle, so that the war seemed to have happened many years ago. A tank, nosing up from the corn like a pale grey toad, would already be rusted, ancient; the underside of an overturned carrier exposed intricacies red-brown and clogged like an agricultural machine abandoned for years. Such objects were no longer the contemporary traffic, they were exceptional carcasses; one expected their armour to melt like the armour of crushed beetles, to enter the earth and help fertilise further the green growth in which they were already drowned.

Claeys and his party — two officers and a driver — drove past many of these histories, through miles of such fertile green growth stretching flatly to either side of the straight and endless grey avenues. Presently they entered the out-skirts of a town. This was a cathedral town, not large, not known much — until by virtue of a battle its name now resounded in black letters the size of the capital letters on the maps of whole countries. This name would now ring huge for generations, it would take its part in the hymn of a national glory; such a name had already become sacred, stony, a symbol of valour. Claeys looked about him with

interest — he had never seen the town before, only heard of
the battle and suffered with the soldiers who had taken it
and held it for four hopeful days with the hope dying each
hour until nearly all were dead, hope and soldiers. Now as
they entered the main street, where already the white tram-
trains were hooting, where the pale walls were chipped and
bullet-chopped, where nevertheless there had never been
the broad damage of heavy bombs and where therefore the
pavements and shop-fronts were already washed and civil
— as they entered these streets decked with summer dresses
and flecked with leaf patterns, Claeys looked in vain for the
town of big letters, and smelled only perfume; a wall of
perfume; they seemed to have entered a scent-burg, a sissy-
burg, a town of female essences, Grasse — but it was only
that this town happened to be planted with lime-trees, lime-
trees everywhere, and these limes were all in flower, their
shaded greenery alive with the golden powdery flower,
whose essence drifted down to the streets and filled them.
The blood was gone, the effort of blood had evaporated.
Only scent, flowers, sunlight, trams, white dresses.

"A nice memorial," Claeys thought. "Keep it in the geogra-
phy book." Then the car stopped outside a barracks. The
officers got out. Claeys said he would wait in the car. He
was not in uniform, he was on a civil mission, attached
temporarily to the army. It does not matter what mission.
It was never fulfilled. All that need be said is that Claeys
was a teacher, engaged then on relief measures, a volunteer
for this work of rehabilitation of the enemy, perhaps a sort
of half-brother-of-mercy as during the occupation he had
been a sort of half-killer. Now he wanted to construct
quickly the world of which he had dreamed during the
shadow years; now he was often as impatient of inaction
as he had learned to be patient before. Patience bends before promise: perhaps this curiosity for spheres of action

quickened his interest as now a lorry-load of soldiers drew up and jumped down at the barrack-gate. One of the soldiers said: "They're using mortars." Another was saying: "And do you blame 'em?"

There had been trouble, they told Claeys, up at the camp for expatriates — the camp where forced labourers imported from all over Europe waited for shipment home. A group of these had heard that a released German prisoner-of-war was returning to work his farm in the vicinity of the camp. They had decided to raid the farm at nightfall, grab as much food as possible, teach the German a trick or two. But the German had somehow got hold of a grenade — from the fields, or perhaps hidden in the farmhouse. At any rate, he had thrown it and killed two of the expatriates. The others had retreated, the story had spat round, before long the expatriates were coming back on the farm in full strength. They had rifles and even mortars. The news got back to the occupational military and a piquet had been sent over. The mortars were opening fire as it arrived: but they were stopped, the expatriates respected the British. Yet to maintain this respect they had to keep a piquet out there for the night. Not all the polskis or czechskis or whoever they were had gone home. A few had hung about, grumbling. The air was by no means clear.

When the officers returned, Claeys told them that he had altered his plans, he wanted to go up and take a look at this expatriates' camp. He gave no reason, and it is doubtful whether he had then a special reason; he felt only that he ought to see these expatriates and talk to them. He had no idea of what to say, but something of the circumstances might suggest a line later.

So they drove out into the country again, into the green. Rich lucent corn stretched endlessly to either side of the straight and endless road. Regularly, in perfect order, precisely intervalled beeches flashed by: a rich, easy, discreet roof of leaves shaded their passage as the foliage met high above. Occasionally a notice at the roadside reminded them of mines uncleared beyond the verges, occasionally a tree bore an orderly white notice addressed to civil traffic. And occasionally a unit of civil traffic passed — a family wheeling a handcart, a cyclist and his passenger, and once a slow-trudging German soldier making his grey way back along the long road to his farm. But there was nothing about this figure in grey-green to suggest more than a farmer dressed as a soldier; he walked slowly, he seemed to be thinking slowly, secure in his destination and free of time as any countryman walking slowly home on an empty road.

All was order. Birds, of course, sang. A green land, unbelievably quiet and rich, sunned its moisture. Each square yard lay unconcerned with the next, just as each measure of the road lay back as they passed, unconcerned with their passing, contented, remaining where it had always been under its own beech, a piece of land. And when at last the beech-rows stopped, the whole of that flat country seemed to spread itself suddenly open. The sky appeared, blue and sailing small white clouds to give it air. Those who deny the flatlands forget the sky — over flat country the sky approaches closer than anywhere else, it takes shape, it becomes the blue-domed lid on a flat plate of earth. Here is a greater intimacy between the elements; and for once, for a little, the world appears finite.

The carload of four travelled like a speck over this flat space. And Claeys was thinking: "Such a summer, such still air — something like a mother presiding heavily and quietly, while down in her young the little vigours boil and breed . . . air almost solid, a sort of unseen fruit fibre . . . a husk guarding the orderly chaos of the breeding ground. . . ."

Such a strict order seemed indeed to preside within the

intricate anarchy — success and failure, vigorous saplings
from the seeds of good fortune, a pennyworth of gas from
the seeds that fall on stony ground: yet a sum total of what
might appear to be complete achievement, and what on the
human level appears to be peace. And on that level, the only
real level, there appeared — over by the poplar plumes? Or
by the windmill? Or at some flat point among the converged
hedges? — there appeared one scar, a scar of purely human
disorder: over somewhere lay this camp of ten thousand
displaced souls, newly freed but imprisoned still by their
strange environment and by their great expectations born
and then as instantly barred. On the face of it, these seemed
to represent disorder, or at most a residue of disorder. But
was this really so? Would such disorder not have appeared
elsewhere, in similar quantity and under conditions of
apparent order? Were they, perhaps, not anything more
than stony-grounders — the disfavoured residue of an anar-
chic nature never governed directly, only impalpably guided
by more general and less concerned governments? Was it
right to rationalise, to impose order upon such seed, was it
right — or at least, was it sensible? It was right, obviously —
for a brain made to reason is itself a part of nature and it
would be wrong to divert it from its necessitous reasoning.
But right though reason may be, there was no more reason
to put one's faith in the impeccable work of the reasoning
brain than to imagine that any other impressive yet deluded
machine — like, for instance, the parachute seed — should
by its apparent ingenuity succeed. Look at the parachute
seed — this amazing seed actually flies off the insensate
plant-mother! It sails on to the wind! The seed itself hangs
beneath such an intricate parasol, it is carried from the roots
of its mother to land on fertile ground far away and set up
there an emissary generation! And more — when it lands,
this engine is so constructed that draughts inch-close to the

soil drag, drag, drag at the little parachute, so that the seed
beneath actually erodes the earth, digs for itself a little
trench of shelter, buries itself! Amazing! And what if the
clever little seed is borne on the wrong wind to a basin of
basalt?

Claeys was thinking: "The rule of natural anarchy — a
few succeed, many waste and die. No material waste: only
a huge waste of effort. The only sure survival is the survival
of the greater framework that includes the seed and all other
things on the earth — the furious landcrab, the bright young
eskimo, the Antiguan cornbroker — every thing and body
. . . and these thrive and decay and compensate . . . just as
we, on the threshold of some golden age of reason, just as
we are the ones to harness some little nuclear genius, pack
it into neat canisters, store it ready to blow up all those
sunny new clinics when the time comes, the time for
compensation. . . ."

Just then the car drove into a small town on the bank of
a broad river. Instantly, in a matter of yards, the green
withered and the party found themselves abruptly in what
seemed to be some sort of a quarry, dry, dug-about, dust-
pale, slagged up on either side with excavated stones.

It was indeed an excavation; it was of course the street
of a town. This town was dead. It had been bombed by a
thousand aircraft, shelled by an entire corps of artillery, and
then fought through by land soldiers. No houses were left,
no streets. The whole had been churned up, smashed and
jig-sawed down again, with some of the jig-saw pieces left
up-ended — those gaunt walls remaining — and the rest of
the pieces desiccated into mounds and hollows and flats. No
grass grew. The air hung sharp with vaporised dust. A few
new alleys had been bulldozed through; these seemed point-
less, for now there was no traffic, the armies had passed
through, the town was deserted. Somewhere in the centre

Claeys stopped the car. He held up his hand for silence. The four men listened. Throughout that wasted city there was no sound. No distant muttering, no murmur. No lost hammering, no drowned cry. No word, no footstep. No wheels. No wind shifting a branch — for there were no trees. No flapping of torn cloth, this avalanche had covered all the cloth. No birds — but one, a small bird that flew straight over, without singing; above such a desert it moved like a small vulture, a shadow, a bird without destination. Brick, concrete, gravel-dust — with only two shaped objects as far all round as they could see: one, an intestinal engine of fat iron pipes, black and big as an upended lorry, something thrown out of a factory; and leaning on its side a pale copper-green byzantine cupola like a gigantic sweet-kiosk blown over by the wind, the tower fallen from what had been the town church. This — in a town that had been the size of Reading.

Almost reverently, as on sacred ground, they started the car and drove off again. Through the pinkish-white mounds the sound of the motor seemed now to intrude garishly. Claeys wanted only to be out of the place. Again, this destruction seemed to have occurred years before; but now because of the very absence of green, of any life at all, of any reason to believe that people had ever lived there. Not even a torn curtain. They wormed through and soon, as abruptly as before, the country began and as from a season-less pause the summer embraced them once more.

Claeys stood up off his seat to look over the passing hedges. The camp was somewhere near now. The driver said, two kilometres. Surely, Claeys thought, surely with that dead town so near the men in this camp could realise the extent of the upheaval, the need for a pause before their journey could be organised? Surely they must see the dis-ruption, this town, the one-way bridges over every stream far around, the roads pitted and impassable? Yet . . . what real meaning had these evidences? Really, they were too negative to be understood, too much again of something long finished. It was not as if something positive, like an army passing, held up one's own purpose; not even a stream of aircraft, showing that at least somewhere there was an effort and direction. No, over these fields there was nothing, not even the sense of a pause, when something might be restarted; instead a vacuity stretched abroad, a vacuum of human endeavour, with the appalling contrast of this vegetable growth continuing evenly and unconcerned. That was really the comprehensible evidence, this sense of the land and of the essence of life continuing, so that one must wish to be up and walking away, to be off to take part not in a regrowth but in a simple continuation of what had always been. For every immediate moment there was food to be sought, the pleasures of taste to be enjoyed: what was more simple than to walk out and put one's hands on a cap-full of eggs, a pig, a few fat hens? And if a grey uniform intervened, then it was above all a grey uniform, something instinctively obstructive, in no real sense connected with the dead town. The only real sympathy that ever came sometimes to soften the greyness of this grey was a discovery, felt occasionally with senses of wonder and unease, that this uniform went walking and working through its own mined cornfields and sometimes blew itself up — that therefore there must be a man inside it, a farmer more than a soldier. But the grey was mostly an obstruction to the ordinary daily desire for food, for fun, for something to be tasted. The day for these men was definitely a day. It was no twenty-four hours building up to a day in the future when something would happen. No future day had been promised. There was, therefore, no succession of days, no days for ticking off, for passing through and storing in preparation. There were in fact the days themselves, each one a matter for living, each a separate dawning and tasting and setting.

Suddenly Claeys heard singing, a chorus of men's voices. A second later the driver down behind the windshield heard it. He nodded, as though they had arrived. The singing grew louder, intimate — as though it came from round a corner that twisted the road immediately ahead. But it came from a lane just before, it flourished suddenly into a full-throated slavic anthem — and there was the lane crowded with men, some sitting, others marching four abreast out into the road. The car whirred down to a dead halt. The singing wavered and stopped. Claeys saw that the driver had only his left hand on the wheel — his other hand was down gripping the black butt of a revolver at his knee. (He had never done this driving through German crowds earlier.)

"It's not the camp," the driver said. "These are some of them, though. The camp's a kilometre up the road." He kept his eyes scanning slowly up and down the line of men crowding in the lane's entry, he never looked up at Claeys. Then the men came a few paces forward, though they looked scarcely interested. Probably they were pushed forward by the crowd behind, many of whom could not have seen the car, many of whom were still singing.

Claeys stood upright and said: "I'd like to talk to these . . . you drive on, get round the corner and wait. I don't want that military feeling."

The men looked on with mild interest, as though they might have had many better things to do. They looked scarcely "displaced"; they had a self-contained air, an independence. There was no censure in their stare; equally no greeting; nor any love. Their clothes were simple, shirts and greyish trousers and boots: though these were weather-stained, they were not ragged.

Claeys jumped down. An interest seemed to quicken in some of the watching men as they saw how Claeys was dressed — béret, plus-fours, leather jacket. It was because of these clothes that the military in the car gave Claeys no salute as they drove off; also because they disapproved of this kind of nonsense, and this may have been why they neither smiled nor waved, but rather nodded impersonally and whirred off round the corner. They might, for instance, have been dropping Claeys after giving him some sort of a lift.

So that Claeys was left quite alone on the road, standing and smiling at the crowd of expatriates grouped at the entrance to the lane. The car had disappeared. It had driven off the road and round the corner. There, as often happens when a vehicle disappears from view, its noise had seemed to vanish too. Presumably it had stopped. But equally it might have been presumed far away on its journey to the next town.

The men took a pace or two forward, now beginning to form a crescent-shape round Claeys, while Claeys began to speak in English: "Good afternoon, mates. Excuse me, I'm Pieter Claeys — native of Belge." None of the men smiled. They only stared hard at him. They were too absorbed now even to mutter a word between themselves. They were searching for an explanation, a sign that would clarify this stranger. They were unsure, and certainly it seemed unimpressed. "Good afternoon, comrades," Claeys shouted. "Gentlemen, hello!"

Without waiting, for the silence was beginning to weigh, he turned into French. "*Suis Claeys de Belge. Je veux vous aider. Vous permettez — on peut causer un peu?*"

He repeated: *"Peut-être?"* And in the pause while no one answered he looked up and above the heads of these men, feeling that his smile might be losing its first flavour, that somehow an embarrassment might be dissolved if he looked away.

The country again stretched wide and green. Claeys was startled then to see sudden huge shapes of paint-box colour erecting themselves in the distance. But then immediately he saw what they were — the wings and fuselages of broken gliders. They rose like the fins of huge fish, tilted at queer angles, grounded and breathlessly still. Difficult at first to understand, for their shapes were strange and sudden, and of an artifice dangerously like something natural: brightly coloured, they might have been shapes torn from an abstract canvas and stuck wilfully on this green background: or the bright broken toys left by some giant child.

Claeys tried again: *"Gijmijneheeren zijt blijkbaar in moeilijkheden. Ik zou die gaarne vernemen. . . ."*

The Dutch words came ruggedly out with a revival of his first vigour, for Claeys was more used to Dutch and its familiarity brought some ease again to his smile. It brought also a first muttering from the men.

They began to mutter to each other in a Slav-sounding dialect — Polish, Ukrainian, Czech, Russian? — and as this muttering grew it seemed to become an argument. Claeys wanted instantly to make himself clearer, he seemed to have made some headway at last and so now again he repeated the Dutch. This time he nodded, raised his arm in a gesture, even took a pace forward in his enthusiasm. But now one of the men behind began to shout angrily, and would have pushed himself forward shaking his fist — had the others not held him.

It was not clear to Claeys — he felt that the Dutch had

been understood, and yet what he had said was friendly . . .
he began to repeat the words again. Then, half-way through,
he thought of a clearer way. He broke into German. There
was every chance that someone might understand German;
they might have been working here for three years or more;
or anyway it was the obvious second language. ". . . *so bin
ich hier um Ihnen zu hilfen gekommen. Bitte Kameraden,
hören Sie mal*. . . ."

The muttering rose, they were plainly talking — and now
not to each other but to him. The crescent had converged
into a half-circle, these many men with livening faces were
half round him. Claeys stood still. Overhead the summer
sky made its huge dome, under which this small group
seemed to make the pin-point centre. The green quiet
stretched endlessly away to cither side, the painted gliders
stuck up brightly. No traffic.

". . . *bitte ein moment . . . ich bin Freund, Freund,
FREUND* . . ." And as he repeated this word "friend" he
realised what his tongue had been quicker to understand —
that none of his listeners knew the meaning of these German
words. They knew only that he was speaking German, they
knew the intonation well.

He stopped. For a moment, as the men nudged each other
nearer, as the Slav words grew into accusation and impreca-
tion, Claeys' mind fogged up appalled by this muddle, help-
lessly overwhelmed by such absurdity, such disorder and
misunderstanding.

Then, making an effort to clear himself, he shook his head
and looked closely from one man to the other. But the com-
posure had gone: they were all mouths, cyes, anger and
desire — they were no longer independent. And this was
accumulating, breeding itself beyond the men as men. They
had become a crowd.

Knowing that words were of no further use, Claeys did the natural thing — wearily, slowly he raised his arm in a last despairing bid for silence.

An unfortunate gesture. The shouting compounded into one confused roar. One of the men on the edge of the crowd jumped out and swung something in the air — a scythe. It cut Claeys down, and then all the pack of them were on him, kicking, striking, grunting and shouting less.

Claeys must have screamed as the scythe hit him — two shots thundered like two full stops into that muddle, there was an abrupt silence and two men fell forward; and then another shot and the men scattered crying into the lane.

Those three soldiers came running up to Claeys' body. They shot again into the men crowding the lane; but then the men, bottled up in the narrow lane, suddenly turned and raised their arms above their heads. The soldiers held their fire, their particular discipline actuated more strongly than their emotions. Two of them kept their guns alert, gestured the men forward. They came, hands raised, shambling awkwardly. The other officer bent down to Claeys.

He was almost finished, messed with blood and blue-white where the flesh showed. He was breathing, trying to speak; and the officer knelt down on both his knees and raised Claeys' head up. But Claeys never opened his eyes — they were bruised shut, anyway. And no words came from his lips, though the officer lowered his head and listened very carefully.

Through the pain, through his battered head, one thought muddled out enormously. "Mistake . . . mistake. . . ." And this split into two other confused, unanswered questions, weakening dulling questions. Broadly, if they could have been straightened out, these questions would have been: "Order or Disorder? Those fellows were the victims of an attempt to rule men into an impeccable order, my killing was the result of the worst, that is, the most stupid disorder. . . ."

But he couldn't get the words out, or any like them. Only — weakly, slowly he raised his right hand. He groped for the officer's hand, and the officer knew what he wanted and met the hand with his own in a handshake. Claeys just managed to point at the place where the men had been, where they still were. Then his head sank deep on to his neck. Again the officer knew what he wanted. He rose, his hand still outstretched from Claeys' grasp, like a hand held out by a splint. Then he started over towards the men.

Instinctively, for this hand of his was wet with blood, he wiped it on his tunic as he walked forward. Without knowing this, he raised his hand again into its gesture of greeting. There was a distasteful expression on his face, for he hardly liked such a duty.

So that when he shook hands with the first of the men, proffering to them, in fact, Claeys' handshake, none of these expatriates knew whether the officer was giving them Claeys' hand or whether he had wiped Claeys' gesture away in distaste and was now offering them his congratulation for killing such a common enemy as Claeys.

ETHAN BRAND

By Nathaniel Hawthorne

A Chapter from an Abortive Romance

Bartram the lime-burner, a rough, heavy-looking man, begrimed with charcoal, sat watching his kiln, at nightfall, while his little son played at building houses with the scattered fragments of marble, when, on the hill-side below them, they heard a roar of laughter, not mirthful, but slow, and even solemn, like a wind shaking the boughs of the forest.

"Father, what is that?" asked the little boy, leaving his play, and pressing betwixt his father's knees.

"O, some drunken man, I suppose," answered the lime-burner; "some merry fellow from the bar-room in the village, who dared not laugh loud enough within doors, lest he should blow the roof of the house off. So here he is, shaking his jolly sides at the foot of Graylock."

"But, father," said the child, more sensitive than the obtuse, middle-aged clown, "he does not laugh like a man that is glad. So the noise frightens me!"

"Don't be a fool, child!" cried his father, gruffly. "You will never make a man, I do believe; there is too much of your mother in you. I have known the rustling of a leaf startle you. Hark! Here comes the merry fellow, now. You shall see that there is no harm in him."

Bartram and his little son, while they were talking thus,

sat watching the same lime-kiln that had been the scene of Ethan Brand's solitary and meditative life, before he began his search for the Unpardonable Sin. Many years, as we have seen, had now elapsed, since that portentous night when the IDEA was first developed. The kiln, however, on the mountain-side, stood unimpaired, and was in nothing changed since he had thrown his dark thoughts into the intense glow of its furnace, and melted them, as it were, into the one thought that took possession of his life. It was a rude, round, tower-like structure, about twenty feet high, heavily built of rough stones, and with a hillock of earth heaped about the larger part of its circumference; so that the blocks and fragments of marble might be drawn by cartloads, and thrown in at the top. There was an opening at the bottom of the tower, like an oven-mouth, but large enough to admit a man in a stooping posture, and provided with a massive iron door. With the smoke and jets of flame issuing from the chinks and crevices of this door, which seemed to give admittance into the hill-side, it resembled nothing so much as the private entrance to the infernal regions, which the shepherds of the Delectable Mountains were accustomed to show to pilgrims.

There are many such lime-kilns in that tract of country, for the purpose of burning the white marble which composes a large part of the substance of the hills. Some of them, built years ago, and long deserted, with weeds growing in the vacant round of the interior, which is open to the sky, and grass and wild-flowers rooting themselves into the chinks of the stones, look already like relics of antiquity, and may yet be overspread with the lichens of centuries to come. Others, where the lime-burner still feeds his daily and night-long fire, afford points of interest to the wanderer among the hills, who seats himself on a log of wood or a fragment of marble, to hold a chat with the solitary man. It is a lonesome, and, when the character is inclined to thought, may be an intensely thoughtful occupation; as it proved in the case of Ethan Brand, who had mused to such strange purpose, in days gone by, while the fire in this very kiln was burning.

The man who now watched the fire was of a different order, and troubled himself with no thoughts save the very few that were requisite to his business. At frequent intervals, he flung back the clashing weight of the iron door, and, turning his face from the insufferable glare, thrust in huge logs of oak, or stirred the immense brands with a long pole. Within the furnace were seen the curling and riotous flames, and the burning marble, almost molten with the intensity of heat; while without, the reflection of the fire quivered on the dark intricacy of the surrounding forest, and showed in the foreground a bright and ruddy little picture of the hut, the spring beside its door, the athletic and coal-begrimed figure of the lime-burner, and the half-frightened child, shrinking into the protection of his father's shadow. And when again the iron door was closed, then reappeared the tender light of the half-full moon, which vainly strove to trace out the indistinct shapes of the neighboring mountains; and, in the upper sky, there was a flitting congregation of clouds, still faintly tinged with the rosy sunset, though thus far down into the valley the sunshine had vanished long and long ago.

The little boy now crept still closer to his father, as footsteps were heard ascending the hill-side, and a human form thrust aside the bushes that clustered beneath the trees.

"Halloo! who is it?" cried the lime-burner, vexed at his son's timidity, yet half infected by it. "Come forward, and show yourself, like a man, or I'll fling this chunk of marble at your head!"

"You offer me a rough welcome," said a gloomy voice, as the unknown man drew nigh. "Yet I neither claim nor desire a kinder one, even at my own fire-side."

To obtain a distincter view, Bartram threw open the iron door of the kiln, whence immediately issued a gush of fierce light, that smote full upon the stranger's face and figure. To a careless eye there appeared nothing very remarkable in his aspect, which was that of a man in a coarse, brown, country-made suit of clothes, tall and thin, with the staff and heavy shoes of a wayfarer. As he advanced, he fixed his eyes — which were very bright — intently upon the brightness of the furnace, as if he beheld, or expected to behold, some object worthy of note within it.

"Good evening, stranger," said the lime-burner; "whence come you, so late in the day?"

"I come from my search," answered the wayfarer; "for, at last, it is finished."

"Drunk! — or crazy!" muttered Bartram to himself. "I shall have trouble with the fellow. The sooner I drive him away, the better."

The little boy, all in a tremble, whispered to his father, and begged him to shut the door of the kiln, so that there might not be so much light; for that there was something in the man's face which he was afraid to look at, yet could not look away from. And, indeed, even the lime-burner's dull and torpid sense began to be impressed by an indescribable something in that thin, rugged, thoughtful visage, with the grizzled hair hanging wildly about it, and those deeply-sunken eyes, which gleamed like fires within the entrance of a mysterious cavern. But, as he closed the door, the stranger turned towards him, and spoke in a quiet, familiar way, that made Bartram feel as if he were a sane and sensible man, after all.

"Your task draws to an end, I see," said he. "This marble has already been burning three days. A few hours more will convert the stone to lime."

"Why, who are you?" exclaimed the lime-burner. "You seem as well acquainted with my business as I am myself."

"And well I may be," said the stranger; "for I followed the same craft many a long year, and here, too, on this very spot. But you are a new-comer in these parts. Did you never hear of Ethan Brand?"

"The man that went in search of the Unpardonable Sin?" asked Bartram, with a laugh.

"The same," answered the stranger. "He has found what he sought, and therefore he comes back again."

"What! then you are Ethan Brand himself?" cried the lime-burner, in amazement. "I am a new-comer here, as you say, and they call it eighteen years since you left the foot of Graylock. But, I can tell you, the good folks still talk about Ethan Brand, in the village yonder, and what a strange errand took him away from his lime-kiln. Well, and so you have found the Unpardonable Sin?"

"Even so!" said the stranger, calmly.

"If the question is a fair one," proceeded Bartram, "where might it be?"

Ethan Brand laid his finger on his own heart.

"Here!" replied he.

And then, without mirth in his countenance, but as if moved by an involuntary recognition of the infinite absurdity of seeking throughout the world for what was the closest of all things to himself, and looking into every heart, save his own, for what was hidden in no other breast, he broke into a laugh of scorn. It was the same slow, heavy laugh, that had almost appalled the lime-burner when it heralded the wayfarer's approach.

The solitary mountain-side was made dismal by it. Laughter, when out of place, mistimed, or bursting forth from a disordered state of feeling, may be the most terrible modulation of the human voice. The laughter of one asleep, even if it be a little child, — the madman's laugh, — the wild, screaming laugh of a born idiot, — are sounds that we sometimes tremble to hear, and would always willingly forget. Poets have imagined no utterance of fiends or hobgoblins so fearfully appropriate as a laugh. And even the obtuse lime-burner felt his nerves shaken, as this strange man looked inward at his own heart, and burst into laughter that rolled away into the night, and was indistinctly reverberated among the hills.

"Joe," said he to his little son, "scamper down to the tavern in the village, and tell the jolly fellows there that Ethan Brand has come back, and that he has found the Unpardonable Sin!"

The boy darted away on his errand, to which Ethan Brand made no objection, nor seemed hardly to notice it. He sat on a log of wood, looking steadfastly at the iron door of the kiln. When the child was out of sight, and his swift and light footsteps ceased to be heard treading first on the fallen leaves and then on the rocky mountain-path, the lime-burner began to regret his departure. He felt that the little fellow's presence had been a barrier between his guest and himself, and that he must now deal, heart to heart, with a man who, on his own confession, had committed the one only crime for which Heaven could afford no mercy. That crime, in its indistinct blackness, seemed to over-shadow him. The lime-burner's own sins rose up within him, and made his memory riotous with a throng of evil shapes that asserted their kindred with the Master Sin, whatever it might be, which it was within the scope of man's corrupted nature to conceive and cherish. They were all of one family; they went to and fro between his breast and Ethan Brand's, and carried dark greetings from one to the other.

Then Bartram remembered the stories which had grown traditionary in reference to this strange man, who had come upon him like a shadow of the night, and was making himself at home in his old place, after so long absence that the dead people, dead and buried for years, would have had more right to be at home, in any familiar spot, than he. Ethan Brand, it was said, had conversed with Satan himself in the lurid blaze of this very kiln. The legend had been matter of mirth heretofore, but looked grisly now. According to this tale, before Ethan Brand departed on his search, he had been accustomed to evoke a fiend from the hot furnace of the lime-kiln, night after night, in order to confer with him about the Unpardonable Sin; the man and the fiend each laboring to frame the image of some mode of guilt which could neither be atoned for nor forgiven. And, with the first gleam of light upon the mountain-top, the fiend crept in at the iron door, there to abide the intensest element of fire, until again summoned forth to share in the dreadful task of extending man's possible guilt beyond the scope of Heaven's else infinite mercy.

While the lime-burner was struggling with the horror of these thoughts, Ethan Brand rose from the log, and flung open the door of the kiln. The action was in such accordance with the idea in Bartram's mind, that he almost expected to see the Evil One issue forth, red-hot from the raging furnace.

"Hold! hold!" cried he, with a tremulous attempt to laugh; for he was ashamed of his fears, although they overmastered him. "Don't, for mercy's sake, bring out your devil now!"

"Man!" sternly replied Ethan Brand, "what need have I of the devil? I have left him behind me, on my track. It is with such half-way sinners as you that he busies himself. Fear not, because I open the door. I do but act by old custom, and am going to trim your fire, like a lime-burner, as I was once."

He stirred the vast coals, thrust in more wood, and bent forward to gaze into the hollow prison-house of the fire, regardless of the fierce glow that reddened upon his face. The lime-burner sat watching him, and half suspected his strange guest of a purpose, if not to evoke a fiend, at least to plunge bodily into the flames, and thus vanish from the sight of man. Ethan Brand, however, drew quietly back, and closed the door of the kiln.

"I have looked," said he, "into many a human heart that was seven times hotter with sinful passions than yonder furnace is with fire. But I found not there what I sought. No, not the Unpardonable Sin!"

"What is the Unpardonable Sin?" asked the lime-burner; and then he shrank further from his companion, trembling lest his question should be answered.

"It is a sin that grew within my own breast," replied Ethan Brand, standing erect, with a pride that distinguishes all enthusiasts of his stamp. "A sin that grew nowhere else! The sin of an intellect that triumphed over the sense of brotherhood with man and reverence for God, and sacrificed everything to its own mighty claims! The only sin that deserves a recompense of immortal agony! Freely, were it to do again, would I incur the guilt. Unshrinkingly I accept the retribution!"

"The man's head is turned," muttered the lime-burner to himself. "He may be a sinner, like the rest of us, — nothing more likely, — but, I'll be sworn, he is a madman too."

Nevertheless he felt uncomfortable at his situation, alone with Ethan Brand on the wild mountain-side, and was right glad to hear the rough murmur of tongues, and the footsteps

of what seemed a pretty numerous party, stumbling over
the stones and rustling through the underbrush. Soon appeared the whole lazy regiment that was wont to infest the
village tavern, comprehending three or four individuals who
had drunk flip beside the bar-room fire through all the
winters, and smoked their pipes beneath the stoop through
all the summers, since Ethan Brand's departure. Laughing
boisterously, and mingling all their voices together in uncere-
monious talk, they now burst into the moonshine and narrow
streaks of fire-light that illuminated the open space before
the lime-kiln. Bartram set the door ajar again, flooding the
spot with light, that the whole company might get a fair
view of Ethan Brand, and he of them.

There, among other old acquaintances, was a once ubiqui-
tous man, now almost extinct, but whom we were formerly
sure to encounter at the hotel of every thriving village
throughout the country. It was the stage-agent. The present
specimen of the genus was a wilted and smoke-dried man,
wrinkled and red-nosed, in a smartly-cut, brown, bob-tailed
coat, with brass buttons, who, for a length of time unknown,
had kept his desk and corner in the bar-room, and was still
puffing what seemed to be the same cigar that he had lighted
twenty years before. He had great fame as a dry joker,
though, perhaps, less on account of any intrinsic humor than
from a certain flavor of brandy-toddy and tobacco-smoke,
which impregnated all his ideas and expressions, as well as
his person. Another well-remembered though strangely
altered face was that of Lawyer Giles, as people still called
him in courtesy; an elderly ragamuffin, in his soiled shirt-
sleeves and tow-cloth trousers. This poor fellow had been an
attorney, in what he called his better days, a sharp practi-
tioner, and in great vogue among the village litigants; but
flip, and sling, and toddy, and cocktails, imbibed at all hours,
morning, noon and night, had caused him to slide from

the courage
spirit of a man

intellectual to various kinds and degrees of bodily labor, till, at last, to adopt his own phrase, he slid into a soap-vat. In other words, Giles was now a soap-boiler, in a small way. He had come to be but the fragment of a human being, a part of one foot having been chopped off by an axe, and an entire hand torn away by the devilish grip of a steam-engine. Yet, though the corporeal hand was gone, a spiritual member remained; for, stretching forth the stump, Giles steadfastly averred that he felt an invisible thumb and fingers with as vivid a sensation as before the real ones were amputated. A maimed and miserable wretch he was; but one, nevertheless, whom the world could not trample on, and had no right to scorn, either in this or any previous stage of his misfortunes, since he had still kept up the courage and spirit of a man, asked nothing in charity, and with his one hand — and that the left one — fought a stern battle against want and hostile circumstances.

Among the throng, too, came another personage, who, with certain points of similarity to Lawyer Giles, had many more of difference. It was the village doctor; a man of some fifty years, whom, at an earlier period of his life, we introduced as paying a professional visit to Ethan Brand during the latter's supposed insanity. He was now a purple-visaged, rude, and brutal, yet half-gentlemanly figure, with something wild, ruined, and desperate in his talk, and in all the details of his gesture and manners. Brandy possessed this man like an evil spirit, and made him as surly and savage as a wild beast, and as miserable as a lost soul; but there was supposed to be in him such wonderful skill, such native gifts of healing, beyond any which medical science could impart, that society caught hold of him, and would not let him sink out of its reach. So, swaying to and fro upon his horse, and grumbling thick accents at the bedside, he visited all the sick-chambers for miles about among the mountain towns, and sometimes raised a dying man, as it were, by miracle, or quite as often, no doubt, sent his patient to a grave that was dug many a year too soon. The doctor had an everlasting pipe in his mouth, and, as somebody said, in allusion to his habit of swearing, it was always alight with hell-fire.

These three worthies pressed forward, and greeted Ethan Brand each after his own fashion, earnestly inviting him to partake of the contents of a certain black bottle, in which, as they averred, he would find something far better worth seeking for than the Unpardonable Sin. No mind, which has wrought itself by intense and solitary meditation into a high state of enthusiasm, can endure the kind of contact with low and vulgar modes of thought and feeling to which Ethan Brand was now subjected. It made him doubt — and, strange to say, it was a painful doubt — whether he had indeed found the Unpardonable Sin, and found it within himself. The whole question on which he had exhausted life, and more than life, looked like a delusion.

"Leave me," he said bitterly, "ye brute beasts, that have made yourselves so, shrivelling up your souls with fiery liquors! I have done with you. Years and years ago, I groped into your hearts, and found nothing there for my purpose. Get ye gone!"

"Why, you uncivil scoundrel," cried the fierce doctor, "is that the way you respond to the kindness of your best friends? Then let me tell you the truth. You have no more found the Unpardonable Sin than yonder boy Joe has. You are but a crazy fellow, — I told you so twenty years ago, — neither better nor worse than a crazy fellow, and the fit companion of old Humphrey, here!"

He pointed to an old man, shabbily dressed, with long white hair, thin visage, and unsteady eyes. For some years past this aged person had been wandering about among the hills, inquiring of all travelers whom he met for his daughter. The girl, it seemed, had gone off with a company of circus-performers; and occasionally tidings of her came to the village, and fine stories were told of her glittering appearance as she rode on horseback in the ring, or performed marvelous feats on the tight-rope.

The white-haired father now approached Ethan Brand, and gazed unsteadily into his face.

"They tell me you have been all over the earth," said he, wringing his hands with earnestness. "You must have seen my daughter, for she makes a grand figure in the world, and everybody goes to see her. Did she send any word to her old father, or say when she was coming back?"

Ethan Brand's eye quailed beneath the old man's. That daughter, from whom he so earnestly desired a word of greeting, was the Esther of our tale, the very girl whom, with such cold and remorseless purpose, Ethan Brand had made the subject of a psychological experiment, and wasted, absorbed, and perhaps annihilated her soul, in the process.

"Yes," murmured he, turning away from the hoary wanderer; "it is no delusion. There is an Unpardonable Sin!"

While these things were passing, a merry scene was going forward in the area of cheerful light, beside the spring and before the door of the hut. A number of the youth of the village, young men and girls, had hurried up the hill-side, impelled by curiosity to see Ethan Brand, the hero of so many a legend familiar to their childhood. Finding nothing, however, very remarkable in his aspect, — nothing but a sunburnt wayfarer, in plain garb and dusty shoes, who sat looking into the fire, as if he fancied pictures among the coals, — these young people speedily grew tired of observing him. As it happened, there was other amusement at hand. An old German Jew, traveling with a diorama on his back, was passing down the mountain-road towards the vil-

lage just as the party turned aside from it, and, in hopes of
eking out the profits of the day, the showman had kept them
company to the lime-kiln.

"Come, old Dutchman," cried one of the young men,
"let us see your pictures, if you can swear they are worth
looking at!"

"O, yes, Captain," answered the Jew, — whether as a
matter of courtesy or craft, he styled everybody Captain, —
"I shall show you, indeed, some very superb pictures!"

So, placing his box in a proper position, he invited the
young men and girls to look through the glass orifices of the
machine, and proceeded to exhibit a series of the most out-
rageous scratchings and daubings, as specimens of the fine
arts, that ever an itinerant showman had the face to impose
upon his circle of spectators. The pictures were worn out,
moreover, tattered, full of cracks and wrinkles, dingy with
tobacco-smoke, and otherwise in a most pitiable condition.
Some purported to be cities, public edifices, and ruined
castles in Europe; others represented Napoleon's battles and
Nelson's sea-fights; and in the midst of these would be seen
a gigantic, brown, hairy hand, — which might have been
mistaken for the Hand of Destiny, though, in truth, it was
only the showman's, — pointing its forefinger to various
scenes of the conflict, while its owner gave historical illus-
trations. When, with much merriment at its abominable
deficiency of merit, the exhibition was concluded, the German bade little Joe put his head into the box. Viewed
through the magnifying-glasses, the boy's round, rosy visage
assumed the strangest imaginable aspect of an immense
Titanic child, the mouth grinning broadly, and the eyes
and every other feature overflowing with fun at the joke.
Suddenly, however, that merry face turned pale, and its
expression changed to horror, for this easily impressed and

excitable child had become sensible that the eye of Ethan Brand was fixed upon him through the glass.

"You make the little man to be afraid, Captain," said the German Jew, turning up the dark and strong outline of his visage, from his stooping posture. "But look again, and, by chance, I shall cause you to see somewhat that is very fine, upon my word!"

Ethan Brand gazed into the box for an instant, and then starting back, looked fixedly at the German. What had he seen? Nothing, apparently; for a curious youth, who had peeped in almost at the same moment, beheld only a vacant space of canvas.

"I remember you now," muttered Ethan Brand to the showman.

"Ah, Captain," whispered the Jew of Nuremberg, with a dark smile, "I find it to be a heavy matter in my show-box, — this Unpardonable Sin! By my faith, Captain, it has wearied my shoulders, this long day, to carry it over the mountain."

"Peace," answered Ethan Brand, sternly, "or get thee into the furnace yonder!"

The Jew's exhibition had scarcely concluded, when a great, elderly dog, — who seemed to be his own master, as no person in the company laid claim to him, — saw fit to render himself the object of public notice. Hitherto, he had shown himself a very quiet, well-disposed old dog, going round from one to another, and, by way of being sociable, offering his rough head to be patted by any kindly hand that would take so much trouble. But now, all of a sudden, this grave and venerable quadruped, of his own mere motion, and without the slightest suggestion from anybody else, began to run round after his tail, which, to heighten the absurdity of the proceeding, was a great deal shorter than

it should have been. Never was seen such headlong eager-
ness in pursuit of an object that could not possibly be
attained; never was heard such a tremendous outbreak of
growling, snarling, barking, and snapping, — as if one end
of the ridiculous brute's body were at deadly and most
unforgivable enmity with the other. Faster and faster, round
about went the cur; and faster and still faster fled the un-
approachable brevity of his tail; and louder and fiercer grew
his yells of rage and animosity; until, utterly exhausted, and
as far from the goal as ever, the foolish old dog ceased his
performance as suddenly as he had begun it. The next
moment he was as mild, quiet, sensible, and respectable in
his deportment, as when he first scraped acquaintance with
the company.

As may be supposed, the exhibition was greeted with
universal laughter, clapping of hands, and shouts of encore,
to which the canine performer responded by wagging all
that there was to wag of his tail, but appeared totally unable
to repeat his very successful effort to amuse the spectators.

Meanwhile, Ethan Brand had resumed his seat upon the
log, and moved, it might be, by a perception of some remote
analogy between his own case and that of this self-pursuing
cur, he broke into the awful laugh, which, more than any
other token, expressed the condition of his inward being.
From that moment, the merriment of the party was at an
end; they stood aghast, dreading lest the inauspicious sound
should be reverberated around the horizon, and that mountain would thunder it to mountain, and so the horror be
prolonged upon their ears. Then, whispering one to another
that it was late, — that the moon was almost down, — that
the August night was growing chill, — they hurried home-
wards, leaving the lime-burner and little Joe to deal as they
might with their unwelcome guest. Save for these three
human beings, the open space on the hill-side was a soli-

tude, set in a vast gloom of forest. Beyond that darksome verge, the fire-light glimmered on the stately trunks and almost black foliage of pines, intermixed with the lighter verdure of sapling oaks, maples, and poplars, while here and there lay the gigantic corpses of dead trees, decaying on the leaf-strewn soil. And it seemed to little Joe — a timorous and imaginative child — that the silent forest was holding its breath, until some fearful thing should happen.

Ethan Brand thrust more wood into the fire, and closed the door of the kiln; then looking over his shoulder at the lime-burner and his son, he bade, rather than advised, them to retire to rest.

"For myself, I cannot sleep," said he. "I have matters that it concerns me to meditate upon. I will watch the fire, as I used to do in the old time."

"And call the devil out of the furnace to keep you company, I suppose," muttered Bartram, who had been making intimate acquaintance with the black bottle above-mentioned. "But watch, if you like, and call as many devils as you like! For my part, I shall be all the better for a snooze. Come, Joe!"

As the boy followed his father into the hut, he looked back at the wayfarer, and the tears came into his eyes, for his tender spirit had an intuition of the bleak and terrible loneliness in which this man had enveloped himself.

When they had gone, Ethan Brand sat listening to the crackling of the kindled wood, and looking at the little spirts of fire that issued through the chinks of the door. These trifles, however, once so familiar, had but the slightest hold of his attention, while deep within his mind he was reviewing the gradual but marvellous change that had been wrought upon him by the search to which he had devoted himself. He remembered how the night dew had fallen upon him, — how the dark forest had whispered to him, — how the stars had gleamed upon him, — a simple and loving man, watching his fire in the years gone by, and ever musing as it burned. He remembered with what tenderness, with what love and sympathy for mankind, and what pity for human guilt and woe, he had first begun to contemplate those ideas which afterwards became the inspiration of his life; with what reverence he had then looked into the heart of man, viewing it as a temple originally divine, and, however desecrated, still to be held sacred by a brother; with what awful fear he had deprecated the success of his pursuit, and prayed that the Unpardonable Sin might never be revealed to him. Then ensued that vast intellectual development, which, in its progress, disturbed the counterpoise between his mind and heart. The Idea that possessed his life had operated as a means of education; it had gone on cultivating his powers to the highest point of which they were susceptible; it had raised him from the level of an unlettered laborer to stand on a star-lit eminence, whither the philosophers of the earth, laden with the lore of universities, might vainly strive to clamber after him. So much for the intellect! But where was the heart? That, indeed, had withered — had contracted — had hardened — had perished! It had ceased to partake of the universal throb. He had lost his hold of the magnetic chain of humanity. He was no longer a brother-man, opening the chambers or the dungeons of our common nature by the key of holy sympathy, which gave him a right to share in all its secrets; he was now a cold observer, looking on mankind as the subject of his experiment, and, at length, converting man and woman to be his puppets, and pulling the wires that moved them to such degrees of crime as were demanded for his study.

Thus Ethan Brand became a fiend. He began to be so from the moment that his moral nature had ceased to keep the pace of improvement with his intellect. And now, as his highest effort and inevitable development, — as the bright and gorgeous flower, and rich, delicious fruit of his life's labor, — he had produced the Unpardonable Sin!

"What more have I to seek? What more to achieve?" said Ethan Brand to himself. "My task is done, and well done!"

Starting from the log with a certain alacrity in his gait, and ascending the hillock of earth that was raised against the stone circumference of the lime-kiln, he thus reached the top of the structure. It was a space of perhaps ten feet across, from edge to edge, presenting a view of the upper surface of the immense mass of broken marble with which the kiln was heaped. All these innumerable blocks and fragments of marble were red-hot and vividly on fire, sending up great spouts of blue flame, which quivered aloft and danced madly, as within a magic circle, and sank and rose again, with continual and multitudinous activity. As the lonely man bent forward over this terrible body of fire, the blasting heat smote up against his person with a breath that, it might be supposed, would have scorched and shrivelled him up in a moment.

Ethan Brand stood erect, and raised his arms on high. The blue flames played upon his face, and imparted the wild and ghastly light which alone could have suited its expression; it was that of a fiend on the verge of plunging into his gulf of intensest torment.

"O Mother Earth," cried he, "who art no more my Mother, and into whose bosom this frame shall never be resolved! O mankind, whose brotherhood I have cast off, and trampled thy great heart beneath my feet! O stars of heaven, that shone on me of old, as if to light me onward and upward! — farewell all, and forever. Come, deadly element of Fire, — henceforth my familiar friend! Embrace me, as I do thee!"

That night the sound of a fearful peal of laughter rolled heavily through the sleep of the lime-burner and his little

son; dim shapes of horror and anguish haunted their dreams,
and seemed still present in the rude hovel, when they opened
their eyes to the daylight.

"Up, boy, up!" cried the lime-burner, staring about him.
"Thank Heaven, the night is gone, at last; and rather than
pass such another, I would watch my lime-kiln, wide awake,
for a twelvemonth. This Ethan Brand, with his humbug of
an Unpardonable Sin, has done me no such mighty favor,
in taking my place!"

He issued from the hut, followed by little Joe, who kept
fast hold of his father's hand. The early sunshine was already
pouring its gold upon the mountain-tops; and though the
valleys were still in shadow, they smiled cheerfully in the
promise of the bright day that was hastening onward. The
village, completely shut in by hills, which swelled away
gently about it, looked as if it had rested peacefully in the
hollow of the great hand of Providence. Every dwelling was
distinctly visible; the little spires of the two churches pointed
upwards, and caught a fore-glimmering of brightness from
the sun-gilt skies upon their gilded weathercocks. The tavern
was astir, and the figure of the old, smoke-dried stage-agent,
cigar in mouth, was seen beneath the stoop. Old Graylock
was glorified with a golden cloud upon his head. Scattered
likewise over the breasts of the surrounding mountains, there
were heaps of hoary mist, in fantastic shapes, some of them
far down into the valley, others high up towards the sum-
mits, and still others, of the same family of mist or cloud,
hovering in the gold radiance of the upper atmosphere.
Stepping from one to another of the clouds that rested on
the hills, and thence to the loftier brotherhood that sailed
in air, it seemed almost as if a mortal man might thus ascend
into the heavenly regions. Earth was so mingled with sky
that it was a day-dream to look at it.

To supply that charm of the familiar and homely, which

Nature so readily adopts into a scene like this, the stage-coach was rattling down the mountain-road, and the driver sounded his horn, while echo caught up the notes, and intertwined them into a rich and varied and elaborate harmony, of which the original performer could lay claim to little share. The great hills played a concert among themselves, each contributing a strain of airy sweetness.

Little Joe's face brightened at once.

"Dear father," cried he, skipping cheerily to and fro, "that strange man is gone, and the sky and the mountains all seem glad of it!"

"Yes," growled the lime-burner, with an oath, "but he has let the fire go down, and no thanks to him if five hundred bushels of lime are not spoiled. If I catch the fellow hereabouts again, I shall feel like tossing him into the furnace!"

With his long pole in his hand, he ascended to the top of the kiln. After a moment's pause, he called to his son.

"Come up here, Joe!" said he.

So little Joe ran up the hillock, and stood by his father's side. The marble was all burnt into perfect, snow-white lime. But on its surface, in the midst of the circle, — snow-white too, and thoroughly converted into lime, — lay a human skeleton, in the attitude of a person who, after long toil, lies down to long repose. Within the ribs — strange to say — was the shape of a human heart.

"Was the fellow's heart made of marble?" cried Bartram, in some perplexity at this phenomenon. "At any rate, it is burnt into what looks like special good lime; and, taking all the bones together, my kiln is half a bushel the richer for him."

So saying, the rude lime-burner lifted his pole, and, letting it fall upon the skeleton, the relics of Ethan Brand were crumbled into fragments.

Nurture he still will be the same — alone

A PAINFUL CASE

Shows slice of Dublin life
Technique clearly done don't notice it
Style — The reader wants to interpret
matter fact — casual, under played part

By James Joyce

mr. Duffy you interpret Duffy yearning

Mr. James Duffy lived in Chapelizod because he wished to live as far as possible from the city of which he was a citizen and because he found all the other suburbs of Dublin mean, modern and pretentious. He lived in an old sombre house and from his windows he could look into the disused distillery or upwards along the shallow river on which Dublin is built. The lofty walls of his uncarpeted room were free from pictures. He had himself bought every article of furniture in the room: a black iron bedstead, an iron wash-stand, four cane chairs, a clothes-rack, a coal-scuttle, a fender and irons and a square table on which lay a double desk. A bookcase had been made in an alcove by means of shelves of white wood. The bed was clothed with white bedclothes and a black and scarlet rug covered the foot. A little hand-mirror hung above the wash-stand and during the day a white-shaded lamp stood as the sole ornament of the mantelpiece. The books on the white wooden shelves were arranged from below upwards according to bulk. A complete Wordsworth stood at one end of the lowest shelf and a copy of the _Maynooth Catechism,_ sewn into the cloth cover of a notebook, stood at one end of the top shelf. Writing materials were always on the desk. In the desk lay a manuscript translation of Hauptmann's _Michael Kramer,_

116

the stage directions of which were written in purple ink, and a little sheaf of papers held together by a brass pin. In these sheets a sentence was inscribed from time to time and, in an ironical moment, the headline of an advertisement for *Bile Beans* had been pasted on to the first sheet. On lifting the lid of the desk a faint fragrance escaped — the fragrance of new cedarwood pencils or of a bottle of gum or of an over-ripe apple which might have been left there and forgotten.

Mr. Duffy abhorred anything which betokened physical or mental disorder. A mediaeval doctor would have called him saturnine. His face, which carried the entire tale of his years, was of the brown tint of Dublin streets. On his long and rather large head grew dry black hair and a tawny moustache did not quite cover an unamiable mouth. His cheekbones also gave his face a harsh character; but there was no harshness in the eyes which, looking at the world from under their tawny eyebrows, gave the impression of a man ever alert to greet a redeeming instinct in others but often disappointed. He lived at a little distance from his body, regarding his own acts with doubtful side-glances. He had an odd autobiographical habit which led him to compose in his mind from time to time a short sentence about himself containing a subject in the third person and a predicate in the past tense. He never gave alms to beggars and walked firmly, carrying a stout hazel.

He had been for many years cashier of a private bank in Baggot Street. Every morning he came in from Chapelizod by tram. At midday he went to Dan Burke's and took his lunch — a bottle of lager beer and a small trayful of arrow-root biscuits. At four o'clock he was set free. He dined in an eating-house in George's Street where he felt himself safe from the society of Dublin's gilded youth and where there was a certain plain honesty in the bill of fare. His evenings were spent either before his landlady's piano or roaming

electing

about the outskirts of the city. His liking for Mozart's music
brought him sometimes to an opera or a concert: these were
the only dissipations of his life.

He had neither companions nor friends, church nor creed.
He lived his spiritual life without any communion with
others, visiting his relatives at Christmas and escorting them
to the cemetery when they died. He performed these two
social duties for old dignity's sake but conceded nothing
further to the conventions which regulate the civic life. He
allowed himself to think that in certain circumstances he
would rob his bank but, as these circumstances never arose,
his life rolled out evenly — an adventureless tale.

One evening he found himself sitting beside two ladies in
the Rotunda. The house, thinly peopled and silent, gave
distressing prophecy of failure. The lady who sat next him
looked round at the deserted house once or twice and then
said:

"What a pity there is such a poor house to-night! It's so
hard on people to have to sing to empty benches."

He took the remark as an invitation to talk. He was surprised that she seemed so little awkward. While they talked
he tried to fix her permanently in his memory. When he
learned that the young girl beside her was her daughter he
judged her to be a year or so younger than himself. Her face,
which must have been handsome, had remained intelligent.
It was an oval face with strongly marked features. The eyes
were very dark blue and steady. Their gaze began with a
defiant note but was confused by what seemed a deliberate
swoon of the pupil into the iris, revealing for an instant a
temperament of great sensibility. The pupil reasserted itself
quickly, this half-disclosed nature fell again under the reign
of prudence, and her astrakhan jacket, moulding a bosom
of a certain fullness, struck the note of defiance more
definitely.

He met her again a few weeks afterwards at a concert in Earlsfort Terrace and seized the moments when her daughter's attention was diverted to become intimate. She alluded once or twice to her husband but her tone was not such as to make the allusion a warning. Her name was Mrs. Sinico. Her husband's great-great-grandfather had come from Leghorn. Her husband was captain of a mercantile boat plying between Dublin and Holland; and they had one child.

Meeting her a third time by accident he found courage to make an appointment. She came. This was the first of many meetings; they met always in the evening and chose the most quiet quarters for their walks together. Mr. Duffy, however, had a distaste for underhand ways and, finding that they were compelled to meet stealthily, he forced her to ask him to her house. Captain Sinico encouraged his visits, thinking that his daughter's hand was in question. He had dismissed his wife so sincerely from his gallery of pleasures that he did not suspect that anyone else would take an interest in her. As the husband was often away and the daughter out giving music lessons Mr. Duffy had many opportunities of enjoying the lady's society. Neither he nor she had had any such adventure before and neither was conscious of any incongruity. Little by little he entangled his thoughts with hers. He lent her books, provided her with ideas, shared his intellectual life with her. She listened to all.

Sometimes in return for his theories she gave out some fact of her own life. With almost maternal solicitude she urged him to let his nature open to the full: she became his confessor. He told her that for some time he had assisted at the meetings of an Irish Socialist Party where he had felt himself a unique figure amidst a score of sober workmen in a garret lit by an inefficient oil-lamp. When the party had divided into three sections, each under its own leader and in its own garret, he had discontinued his attendances. The workmen's discussions, he said, were too timorous; the interest they took in the question of wages was inordinate. He felt that they were hard-featured realists and that they resented an exactitude which was the produce of a leisure not within their reach. No social revolution, he told her, would be likely to strike Dublin for some centuries.

She asked him why did he not write out his thoughts. For what, he asked her, with careful scorn. To compete with phrasemongers, incapable of thinking consecutively for sixty seconds? To submit himself to the criticisms of an obtuse middle class which entrusted its morality to policemen and its fine arts to impresarios?

He went often to her little cottage outside Dublin; often they spent their evenings alone. Little by little, as their thoughts entangled, they spoke of subjects less remote. Her companionship was like a warm soil about an exotic. Many times she allowed the dark to fall upon them, refraining from lighting the lamp. The dark discreet room, their isolation, the music that still vibrated in their ears united them. This union exalted him, wore away the rough edges of his character, emotionalised his mental life. Sometimes he caught himself listening to the sound of his own voice. He thought that in her eyes he would ascend to an angelical stature; and, as he attached the fervent nature of his companion more and more closely to him, he heard the strange impersonal voice which he recognized as his own, insisting on the soul's incurable loneliness. We cannot give ourselves, it said: we are our own. The end of these discourses was that one night during which she had shown every sign of unusual excitement, Mrs. Sinico caught up his hand passionately and pressed it to her cheek.

Mr. Duffy was very much surprised. Her interpretation of his words disillusioned him. He did not visit her for a week; then he wrote to her asking her to meet him. As he did not wish their last interview to be troubled by the influence of their ruined confessional they met in a little cakeshop near the Parkgate. It was cold autumn weather but in spite of the cold they wandered up and down the roads of the Park for nearly three hours. They agreed to break off their intercourse: every bond, he said, is a bond to sorrow. When they came out of the Park they walked in silence towards the tram; but here she began to tremble so violently that, fearing another collapse on her part, he bade her good-bye quickly and left her. A few days later he received a parcel containing his books and music.

Four years passed. Mr. Duffy returned to his even way of life. His room still bore witness of the orderliness of his mind. Some new pieces of music encumbered the music-stand in the lower room and on his shelves stood two volumes by Nietzsche: *Thus Spake Zarathustra* and *The Gay Science*. He wrote seldom in the sheaf of papers which lay in his desk. One of his sentences, written two months after his last interview with Mrs. Sinico, read: Love between man and man is impossible because there must not be sexual intercourse and friendship between man and woman is impossible because there must be sexual intercourse. He kept away from concerts lest he should meet her. His father died; the junior partner of the bank retired. And still every morning he went into the city by tram and every evening walked home from the city after having dined moderately in George's Street and read the evening paper for dessert.

One evening as he was about to put a morsel of corned beef and cabbage into his mouth his hand stopped. His eyes fixed themselves on a paragraph in the evening paper which he had propped against the water-carafe. He replaced the morsel of food on his plate and read the paragraph attentively. Then he drank a glass of water, pushed his plate to

one side, doubled the paper down before him between his
elbows and read the paragraph over and over again. The
cabbage began to deposit a cold white grease on his plate.
The girl came over to him to ask was his dinner not properly
cooked. He said it was very good and ate a few mouthfuls
of it with difficulty. Then he paid his bill and went out.

He walked along quickly through the November twilight,
his stout hazel stick striking the ground regularly, the fringe
of the buff *Mail* peeping out of a side-pocket of his tight
reefer overcoat. On the lonely road which leads from the
Parkgate to Chapelizod he slackened his pace. His stick
struck the ground less emphatically and his breath, issuing
irregularly, almost with a sighing sound, condensed in the
wintry air. When he reached his house he went up at once
to his bedroom and, taking the paper from his pocket, read
the paragraph again by the failing light of the window. He
read it not aloud, but moving his lips as a priest does when
he reads the prayers *Secreto*. This was the paragraph:

DEATH OF A LADY AT SYDNEY PARADE

A PAINFUL CASE

To-day at the City of Dublin Hospital the Deputy Coroner
(in the absence of Mr. Leverett) held an inquest on the
body of Mrs. Emily Sinico, aged forty-three years, who was
killed at Sydney Parade Station yesterday evening. The evidence showed that the deceased lady, while attempting to
cross the line, was knocked down by the engine of the ten
o'clock slow train from Kingstown, thereby sustaining injuries of the head and right side which led to her death.

James Lennon, driver of the engine, stated that he had
been in the employment of the railway company for fifteen
years. On hearing the guard's whistle he set the train in
motion and a second or two afterwards brought it to rest in
response to loud cries. The train was going slowly.

P. Dunne, railway porter, stated that as the train was about to start he observed a woman attempting to cross the lines. He ran towards her and shouted, but, before he could reach her, she was caught by the buffer of the engine and fell to the ground.

A Juror. "You saw the lady fall?"

Witness. "Yes."

Police-Sergeant Croly deposed that when he arrived he found the deceased lying on the platform apparently dead. He had the body taken to the waiting-room pending the arrival of the ambulance.

Constable 57 corroborated.

Dr. Halpin, assistant house-surgeon of the City of Dublin Hospital, stated that the deceased had two lower ribs fractured and had sustained severe contusions of the right shoulder. The right side of the head had been injured in the fall. The injuries were not sufficient to have caused death in a normal person. Death, in his opinion, had been probably due to shock and sudden failure of the heart's action.

Mr. H. B. Patterson Finlay, on behalf of the railway company, expressed his deep regret at the accident. The company had always taken every precaution to prevent people crossing the lines except by the bridges, both by placing notices in every station and by the use of patent spring gates at level crossings. The deceased had been in the habit of crossing the lines late at night from platform to platform and, in view of certain other circumstances of the case, he did not think the railway officials were to blame.

Captain Sinico, of Leoville, Sydney Parade, husband of the deceased, also gave evidence. He stated that the deceased was his wife. He was not in Dublin at the time of the accident as he had arrived only that morning from Rotterdam. They had been married for twenty-two years and had lived happily until about two years ago when his wife began to be rather intemperate in her habits.

Miss Mary Sinico said that of late her mother had been in the habit of going out at night to buy spirits. She, witness, had often tried to reason with her mother and had induced her to join a League. She was not at home until an hour after the accident.

The jury returned a verdict in accordance with the medical evidence and exonerated Lennon from all blame.

The Deputy-Coroner said it was a most painful case, and expressed great sympathy with Captain Sinico and his daughter. He urged on the railway company to take strong measures to prevent the possibility of similar accidents in the future. No blame attached to anyone.

Mr. Duffy raised his eyes from the paper and gazed out of his window on the cheerless evening landscape. The river lay quiet beside the empty distillery and from time to time a light appeared in some house on the Lucan road. What an end! The whole narrative of her death revolted him and it revolted him to think that he had ever spoken to her of what he held sacred. The threadbare phrases, the inane expressions of sympathy, the cautious words of a reporter won over to conceal the details of a commonplace vulgar death attacked his stomach. Not merely had she degraded herself; she had degraded him. He saw the squalid tract of her vice, miserable and malodorous. His soul's companion! He thought of the hobbling wretches whom he had seen carrying cans and bottles to be filled by the barman. Just God, what an end! Evidently she had been unfit to live, without any strength of purpose, an easy prey to habits, one of the wrecks on which civilization has been reared. But that she could have sunk so low! Was it possible he had deceived himself so utterly about her? He remembered her outburst of that night and interpreted it in a harsher sense than he had ever done. He had no difficulty now in approving of the course he had taken.

As the light failed and his memory began to wander he thought her hand touched his. The shock which had first attacked his stomach was now attacking his nerves. He put on his overcoat and hat quickly and went out. The cold air met him on the threshold; it crept into the sleeves of his coat. When he came to the public-house at Chapelizod Bridge he went in and ordered a hot punch.

The proprietor served him obsequiously but did not venture to talk. There were five or six workingmen in the shop discussing the value of a gentleman's estate in County Kildare. They drank at intervals from their huge pint tumblers and smoked, spitting often on the floor and sometimes dragging the sawdust over their spits with their heavy boots. Mr. Duffy sat on his stool and gazed at them, without seeing or hearing them. After a while they went out and he called for another punch. He sat a long time over it. The shop was very quiet. The proprietor sprawled on the counter reading the *Herald* and yawning. Now and again a tram was heard swishing along the lonely road outside.

As he sat there, living over his life with her and evoking alternately the two images in which he now conceived her, he realized that she was dead, that she had ceased to exist, that she had become a memory. He began to feel ill at ease. He asked himself what else could he have done. He could not have carried on a comedy of deception with her; he could not have lived with her openly. He had done what seemed to him best. How was he to blame? Now that she was gone he understood how lonely her life must have been, sitting night after night alone in that room. His life would be lonely too until he, too, died, ceased to exist, became a memory — if anyone remembered him.

It was after nine o'clock when he left the shop. The night was cold and gloomy. He entered the Park by the first gate and walked along under the gaunt trees. He walked through the bleak alleys where they had walked four years before. She seemed to be near him in the darkness. At moments he seemed to feel her voice touch his ear, her hand touch his. He stood still to listen. Why had he withheld life from her? Why had he sentenced her to death? He felt his moral nature falling to pieces.

When he gained the crest of the Magazine Hill he halted and looked along the river towards Dublin, the lights of which burned redly and hospitably in the cold night. He looked down the slope and, at the base, in the shadow of the wall of the Park, he saw some human figures lying. Those venal and furtive loves filled him with despair. He gnawed the rectitude of his life; he felt that he had been outcast from life's feast. One human being had seemed to love him and he had denied her life and happiness: he had sentenced her to ignominy, a death of shame. He knew that the prostrate creatures down by the wall were watching him and wished him gone. No one wanted him; he was outcast from life's feast. He turned his eyes to the grey gleaming river, winding along towards Dublin. Beyond the river he saw a goods train winding out of Kingsbridge Station, like a worm with a fiery head winding through the darkness, obstinately and laboriously. It passed slowly out of sight; but still he heard in his ears the laborious drone of the engine reiterating the syllables of her name.

He turned back the way he had come, the rhythm of the engine pounding in his ears. He began to doubt the reality of what memory told him. He halted under a tree and allowed the rhythm to die away. He could not feel her near him in the darkness nor her voice touch his ear. He waited for some minutes listening. He could hear nothing: the night was perfectly silent. He listened again: perfectly silent. He felt that he was alone.

HAPPINESS*

By Guy de Maupassant

It was tea-time, the lamps had not yet been brought in. The villa overlooked the sea; the sun as it went down had left the sky a rosy pink, brushed with gold dust, and the Mediterranean, without a ripple, without a tremor, still gleaming under the light of the dying day, was a boundless sheet of polished metal.

In the distance, off to the right, the jagged mountains outlined their black profile against the fading purple of the sunset.

The talk was of love, they were arguing the old subject of endless argument, saying over again things they had said many times before. The gentle melancholy of the twilight made their words slow, brought a tenderness to their souls, and the word "love," returning ceaselessly, now in a man's strong voice, now in a woman's light one, seemed to fill the little salon, to flutter about in it like a bird, to hover over it like a spirit.

Is it possible to stay in love for several years on end?

"Yes," some claimed.

"No," affirmed others.

Distinctions were made, dividing lines were established, examples were cited, and all in the little group, men and

* *Le Bonheur.* (My translation. Ed.)

127

women alike, filled with powerful, disturbing memories which they could not utter but which rose unbidden to their lips, seemed touched with feeling; they spoke of what is at once banal and supremely rare — the tender and mysterious harmony of two beings — with deep emotion and burning interest.

But suddenly one of the men, his eyes fixed on the distance, cried: "Oh! look out there! What can it be?"

On the sea, at the limit of the horizon, there had arisen a huge, dim, gray mass.

The women had stood up and were gazing uncomprehendingly at this amazing phenomenon which they had never seen before.

Someone said: "It's Corsica! You can see it like this two or three times a year under certain unusual atmospheric conditions, when the air is perfectly clear and doesn't hide it in mists and vapor."

They could dimly make out the mountain crests, they thought they could see the snow on the peaks. For a time all were startled, troubled, almost frightened by this sudden apparition of a world, by this phantom arising from the sea. Perhaps such strange visions appeared to those who set out like Columbus to cross unexplored oceans.

Then an old gentleman who had not hitherto spoken declared:

"Wait a moment. On that island which has risen up before us as if to reply to what we have been saying and to bring a strange recollection to my mind — on that island I once witnessed an admirable example of constant love, a love that was happier than one would have believed possible.

"This is the story."

Five years ago I made a trip to Corsica. That savage island is more secret and farther from us than America, even though it is occasionally seen from the coast of France, as we see it today.

Imagine a world still in chaos, a tempest of mountains separating narrow ravines in which torrents roll; no plain, but immense waves of granite and gigantic undulations of ground covered with scrub or with tall forests of chestnut and pine. It is virgin soil, uncultivated, deserted, although one sometimes spies a village, like a heap of rocks, on the summit of a mountain. No cultivation, no industry, no art. One never comes across a bit of carved wood, a fragment of sculptured stone, never the memory of an ancestral taste, childish or refined, for graceful and beautiful things. That is precisely what strikes one most in this superb, hard country: the hereditary indifference towards that pursuit of seductive form which we call art.

Italy, where every palace filled with masterpieces is itself a masterpiece, where marble, wood, bronze, iron, all metals and all stones bear witness to the genius of man, where the smallest antique objects which lie about in the old houses reveal a divine care for grace, Italy is for all of us the sacred fatherland which we love for revealing and affirming to us the effort, the grandeur, the power, and the triumph of the creative intelligence.

And just across from Italy, savage Corsica has remained what it was in its earliest days. The human creature lives there in his rough dwelling, indifferent to everything which does not have a bearing on his own life or on his family quarrels. He has retained the defects and the virtues of uncultivated races, he is violent, full of hatred, bloodthirsty without conscience, but also hospitable, generous, loyal, simple, opening his door to the wayfarer and giving his faithful friendship in return for the slightest mark of sympathy.

So for a month I had been wandering across that magnifi-

cent island, always with the sensation that I was at the end
of the world. No inns, no taverns, no roads. By mule-paths
you reach a hamlet, perched on the side of a mountain,
overlooking a tortuous abyss from which arises, in the evening, the continuous deep, muffled voice of a torrent. You
knock at a door. You ask for a night's lodging and for food
to keep you until the next day. And you sit at the humble
table, sleep under the humble roof; in the morning you
shake the proffered hand of your host, who has gone with
you to the limits of the village.

Now one evening, after ten hours of walking, I came to a
tiny dwelling situated quite by itself at the bottom of a
narrow valley which ran down to the sea a league farther on.
The two steep mountain-sides, covered with scrub, dis-
lodged boulders and great trees, enclosed this mournful
ravine like the gloomy walls of a prison or fortification.

Round about the thatched cottage, a few vines, a small
garden, and farther off a few tall chestnuts: in short, a liveli-
hood — for this poor country a fortune.

The woman who welcomed me was old, severe, and
exceptionally neat. The man, seated on a straw-bottomed
chair, stood up to greet me, then sat down again without
saying a word. His companion said to me: "You must excuse
him; he's deaf now. He is eighty-two years old."

She spoke French as we speak it in France. I was
surprised.

I asked her: "You are not a native of Corsica?"

She replied, "No, we're continentals. But we have lived
here for fifty years."

A feeling of sorrow and fear seized me at the thought
of those fifty years spent in this gloomy place, so far from
the towns of men. An old shepherd came in, and we sat
down to the one dish which constituted dinner, a thick
soup in which potatoes, bacon, and cabbage had been
cooked together.

When the brief meal was over, I went to sit before the door, my heart clutched by the melancholy of the bleak country-side, constrained by the distress which may overcome the traveller on certain sad evenings, in certain desolate places. At such moments something seems to come to an end, existence and the universe together. One is suddenly aware of the terrible misery of life, of the isolation in which we live, of the all-embracing nothingness, of the bleak solitude of the heart obliged to lull and deceive itself with dreams until death.

The old woman joined me and said, tormented by the curiosity which still lives at the bottom of even the most resigned hearts: "So you come from France?"

"Yes, I'm travelling for pleasure."

"You're from Paris, perhaps?"

"No, I'm from Nancy."

It seemed to me that she was seized by an extraordinary emotion. How I saw that, or rather how I sensed it, I do not know.

She repeated slowly: "You are from Nancy?"

The man appeared in the doorway, impassive in the manner of the deaf.

She continued: "It makes no difference. He can't hear."

Then, after a few seconds, "So you know people in Nancy?"

"Why yes, almost everybody."

"The Sainte-Allaize family?"

"Yes, very well; they were friends of my father."

"What is your name?"

I told her my name. She looked at me fixedly, then said, in the low voice with which we speak of memories awakened:

"Yes, yes, I remember. And the Brisemare family, what has become of them?"

"They are all dead."

"Ah! . . . And the Sirmonts, did you know them?"

"Yes, the last of them is a general."

Then she said, trembling with emotion, with anguish, with I know not what confused feeling, powerful and inviolable, with I know not what need to confess, to tell everything, to speak of things which she had hitherto held locked away in the depths of her heart, to speak of the people whose very name convulsed her soul:

"Yes, Henri de Sirmont. I know him well. He is my brother."

Startled and dismayed, I raised my eyes to her face. And suddenly I remembered.

In the old days, it had made a huge scandal in noble Lorraine. A beautiful and wealthy girl, Suzanne de Sirmont, had been carried off by a non-commissioned officer of hussars in the regiment commanded by her father.

The soldier who had captivated the colonel's daughter was a handsome lad, the son of peasants but wearing the hussar's blue dolman none the less well for that. No doubt she had seen him, singled him out, and fallen in love with him as she watched the squadrons parade. But how had he spoken to her, how had they managed to see each other, to reach an understanding, how had she dared to let him know that she loved him? The answers to those questions no one ever knew.

No one had guessed or foreseen anything. One evening, when the soldier had just finished his term of enlistment, he disappeared with her. They were sought, but they were not found. There was never any news of them, and she was considered dead.

And here I had found her, in this sinister valley.

It was my turn to speak: "Yes, I remember very well. You are Mademoiselle Suzanne."

She made a sign, "yes," with her head, her tears falling.

Then, directing my attention by a glance to the old man standing motionless at the threshold of his hovel, she said:

"That is he."

And I understood that she still loved him, that she saw him still with eyes on which he had cast a spell.

I asked, "Have you at least been happy?"

In a voice which came from her heart she answered, "Oh, yes, very happy! He has made me very happy. I have had no regrets."

I looked at her in sadness and surprise, marvelling at the power of love. This daughter of a wealthy family had followed this man, this peasant. She had herself become a peasant. She had adapted herself to his life, a life devoid of charm, lacking all delicacy and luxury, she had stooped to the level of his simple habits. And she still loved him. She had become the wife of a churl, wearing a country bonnet and homespun. Seated on a straw-bottomed chair, she ate a stew of cabbage and bacon and potatoes, from an earthenware dish on a deal table. She slept on a straw tick at his side.

She had never thought of anything but him! She had regretted nothing: not her jewels, nor her gowns, nor the elegant adornments of her former life. She had not missed the luxurious furnishings, nor the perfumed warmth of rooms closed in with hangings, nor the lightness of down on which to rest at night. She had never needed anything but him; as long as he was there, she asked for nothing more.

She had cut herself off, while still a young girl, from life, from society, from those who had reared her and loved her. She had come, alone with him, to this wild ravine. And he had been everything to her, everything we long for, everything we dream of, everything we endlessly wait for and unceasingly hope for. He had filled her life, from one end to the other, with happiness.

She could not have been happier.

All night long, listening to the heavy breathing of the old
soldier on his pallet, I thought of this strange and simple
adventure, of this happiness which was so complete and yet
made of so little.

And I left at sunrise, after shaking the hands of the two
old people.

The story-teller was silent. A woman said:

"All the same, her ideal was too easily attained, her needs
were too primitive and her demands too simple. She must
have been a fool."

Another woman said slowly, "What does it matter! She
was happy."

Out on the horizon Corsica buried itself in the night,
returned slowly into the sea, effaced its huge shadow which
had appeared as if on purpose to tell the story of the two
humble lovers sheltered within its shores.

KEEP YOUR PITY

By Kay Boyle

Va, garde ta pitié comme ton ironie!
MALLARMÉ

Mr. Jefferson was an American, a good and simple man, so he did not see these people as they were: haughty, aloof, almost distasteful in their pride. He did not see them, the two old people, as weird as skeletons jerking down the walk; his eyes swathed them in weakness and frailty, and smoothed out the skin that hung crumpled and soft from their faces. Mr. Jefferson sat on the café terrace and watched them coming down the promenade one morning after another in the sun: colorless in their flesh, with a faint smell of a final spring on them, shaking a little on their limbs as the first pale mimosa flowers quivered on the branch.

It was the sun that brought them forth, making new promises every day to them. He wore a tight-fitting black-and-auburn check, old Mr. Wycherley, and a tan bowler hat, light in color, and he must have been elegant in his time. But now his time was past, or should have been, and there was nothing to be said for the cut of his jacket at the waist, or for the black silk stock that wound glossy around his haggard throat. He was a genteel old man, to the eye, with his wife on his arm, and she with her lids swollen yellow and thin as gauze under her veil, wearing plum velvet and a litter of tiger cats' hides fast on the points of her shoulders.

They had no use for pity, having seen it a common thing in the faces of everyone passing. And there was no need to give it, for they had their own style, their own special wraithlike air amongst the living contemporary people walking by the Mediterranean Sea. No one need have pitied them their transparent hands on their canes, for when they paused to stroke the thin cat near Mr. Jefferson's table they did not speak of its bones or hunger; there was something like mockery or greed in the eye they gave it. They ran their old hands over the links of its spine, touching its knobs curiously, as if for the value of the skin or the real amber in the sockets of its head. Mr. Jefferson witnessed, as a blind man might, this spectacle. He heard their childish, pure voices speaking English, and because they had halted there and stroked the animal, he took for mercy the rapacity of their hearts.

He heard the old lady say in her querulous, pride-bitten way: "It's damnably small, Mr. W."

And the old gentleman answered, quoting in proud, elegant French: " 'Va, garde ta pitié comme ton ironie.' Keep it for yourself, Mrs. W. There's no telling but what you may have need of one or the other someday."

Mr. Jefferson had come the week before to Nice, an American sitting there in his good gray suit, with the unfailing credulous soul of his country lighted in his eye. He was presented by the French people sitting next at the café table where the Wycherleys had paused to speak a moment. They were the Aristocrats, the high-and-mighty old couple, the seemingly frail and gracious pair. They gave a great interest and care to their conversations, and to the conversations of people they exchanged the time of day with, as if some great ear were gaping in space, spying forever on what they had to say. But they never accepted the invitations to sit down on the café terrace, but halted at one table or the next, talking with charm but inscrutably to those they knew, but moving on as if an hour had been fixed elsewhere with someone else who might even now be waiting. Mr. Wycherley held his hat pressed to his linen vest as he spoke. His thin yellowish-white hair was parted to one side and smoothed across, lying listless, as the fingers of a dead man might have lain upon his skull.

They had simply bowed to Mr. Jefferson, but then, a thunderclap to their reason, they felt his hands fall in familiarity upon their arms. The sun was out, and the air melting and fair, but the blast of their horror swept them cold. They stood rooted, their sap standing motionless in their veins and their senses stilled in fright. Before them the American's face was grimacing and urging, as though it would be a gift from their hearts to him if they should bend their brittle knees and take the empty chairs. He did not know what kept them from sitting; he did not know if it was for fear of their antique clothes splitting up the seams, or for fear of what he might do or say.

"You'd be doing me a favor," said Mr. Jefferson gently, "if you'd have a little glass . . ."

But Mr. Wycherley cried out: "Ah, no, sir, we do not drink!"

His bones seemed to buckle and knock in his skin as he stepped back in his pumps and gaiters from Mr. Jefferson's table. His voice ran fast through his smooth shining lips, his head reared on the cords of his neck, and his wild glance smote the stranger's viciously in mistrust. He saw the American as many things, the man sitting there, his eyes a straight unwinking blue behind his big-hewed features, and a little mat of graying hair set up on the top of his head.

"Well, if you'd sit down, then, and have a little talk,"

said Mr. Jefferson, with the slow wistful smile so little
matched to the clanging voice. "I'm new to this country.
I feel like a fish out of water with all this parley-voo."

So after a while they saw it — through their suspicion for
what he might be they saw the accumulated hunger for
speech that sucked away at his clean-shaven jaws. He knew
no one in the city, he said, and this did not touch them,
although they saw his solitude very well. He was famished
for kind words to be spoken to him, and there they stood
listening, warily, giving nothing from their deceptive silence.
He sat talking, with his glass on the table before him, with
no thought of rising in respect, though he was still a young-
ish man, fifty-five or less.

"This is called the city of perfume and flowers," said
Mrs. Wycherley in her frail, wincing voice. She spoke
breathlessly, in caution to him, as a young woman speaking
her marriage vows might do. This was her welcome to Mr.
Jefferson, although she smiled little because of the holes in
the far sides of her mouth where the teeth were missing.

"That's what I'm here for," said Mr. Jefferson. As he talked
they could see the absolute wastes and stretches without
beauty that lay behind him. Strange, strange, the undulations of life given so in a few uneasy sentences to them. They
stood with their eyes bright and callous before the spectacle of his years running quick over impediments and falls,
the narrow, tortuous current of his life passing with difficulty before them, like a stream squeezed hard in its bed.
But now the time for rest had come, he said. Now he could
sit still, if he liked, and watch the waters of his repose lap
in expansion, far, and deep, and wide.

He was from Ohio, and in this way he talked of his home
until they saw, even as much as some details of it, in their
cold perverse hearts. The dust lay three inches deep on the
roads in the summertime, he said, and in winter there was

the cold, and the months of the winter were laid away in the country, sunless and endless.

"And here, sir," said Mr. Wycherley, with his smile in his long old teeth, and his bowler hat pressed over his linen vest, "here, although we are not native sons, we enjoy the native sun!"

Mrs. Wycherley looked slyly at the American and laughed her faint high laughter. But Mr. Jefferson had seemingly not heard, or else not understood. There he sat, thinking of the many years of perseverance that had brought him so far and left him idle there.

"I cleared out of things just in time," he was saying. "I wasn't really hit at all. What I've got put away, I want it to pay me some dividends in real enjoyment now." But there was the wistful, the hopeless longing in his mouth, sorrowing of itself under the hard ringing clamor of his voice. He had worked so hard, gone in the teeth of it for so long, that now there was no place of rest and pleasure left vacant for him any more.

"I built up my business alone," he was saying, not in pride, but in mild complaint to them. "I sold out at a profit this year. Now my time's all my own," he said in sorrow. "All my own." He had no one to share it with. The two old people stood still, eying him with cold, vulturelike, inward eyes.

"Why don't you folks have dinner with me?" Mr. Jefferson said.

Such speech in the mouth of any other man would have sent them off in affront, but this man was speaking out of his own ignorance to them. There was no hesitation in Mr. Wycherley's mind: he knew very well they could never sit down at table with this stranger. He was some kind of court fool, a jester, and they, in their pride, were the royalty in a high, indifferent society of death.

"You're kind indeed, sir," said Mr. Wycherley, bowing.

"I'm afraid we shall have to beg off this time," said the old man, smiling down from his perilous height of race and breeding upon Mr. Jefferson. "Mrs. Wycherley and I have guests to dinner . . ."

"Damn it, I'm hungry," said Mrs. Wycherley, and her underlip went wrinkled and small as if she were about to cry.

"As I was saying," said the old gentleman, and he cleared his throat in rebuke at her, "Mrs. Wycherley and I have guests, as it happens . . ."

They had lived twelve years in the apartment, almost without event, it might be said. But when they came home from their talk with the American, a new thing awaited them. There was a blue notice pasted flat on the wood of their handsome ancient door. Surely some warning must have been given, but although they searched the confusion of their thoughts for it, no memory of it lingered. They had done the four flights at length, with the breath running thin in their lungs, and when they paused, gasping, they saw the blue paper fixed fast to the door.

Mr. Wycherley put his glasses on his nose and began reading it aloud: it said because you have not paid, or because you will not pay, or because you cannot pay the rent for the last quarter and this, everything inside will be laid hold of tomorrow morning at nine o'clock. Mr. Wycherley took out his pocket handkerchief and passed it over his face in haste as if to wipe from his features any signs of fear. Then he began to laugh aloud:

"Ha, ha, ha," said Mr. Wycherley. "Here's a fine one! This is a good joke indeed! I'll have to run over and see Jean Medecin!"

Jean Medecin was the mayor of Nice, and although they did not know him, the sound of his name spoken now lifted their long heavy heads rearing, like a bit in the mouth. But the divinity had faded in Mrs. Wycherley's face, and she stood by his side, shaking.

"Preposterous!" cried Mr. Wycherley sternly to her. Together their minds went back, groping through the uneasy darkness of their memories. Had they paid, or had they not, or why had they not? "Take my arm," said Mr. Wycherley. "This is the most preposterous thing!"

Twelve years, they were thinking, twelve years. They stood quiet, groping slowly back through the confusion, feeling for the corners and grooves of something known in the darkness. And then suddenly Mr. Wycherley touched it and drew it forth tentatively, little by little, to the light.

"The proprietor called in a month ago, didn't he, Mrs. W.?" he said. "Didn't he speak of raising the rent?"

The dew on her brow shone strangely out, supernaturally lucent, yet milky, like mother-of-pearl.

"Herriot shall hear of this," said Mr. Wycherley. Herriot was the mayor of Lyons, and with the strength of that name in their ears they unlocked the door and passed through it, arm in arm together. She had no strength left to put out her hand and lift the edge of her velvet, and it rode in silence and majesty over the threshold's stone.

They proceeded to the bedroom together, with such dignity as if the invisible eye were watching, the unseen ear listening still in space. Here was the garden party to which they had been invited: the false Aubusson over the bed, the paper flowers blooming on the chimney, and the two windows with the shutters drawn in combs of sun. Outside the sun was shining hot and bright on the square named after Garibaldi. The gray coat of a goat or two had been stitched together into a square coarse rug, and it might have been a soiled chrysanthemum discarded there and fading on the floor.

"Now, Mrs. W.," said Mr. Wycherley, "you go to bed, my

dear." She seemed to be slipping, slipping away in bewilderment, with only the hard active bubbles of her eyes riding to the surface of her confusion. She sat on the side of the bed, thinking that the police should never get the goatskin rug, but there seemed no certainty left in her. There she sat, curved and senseless in her velvets, speechless on the Aubusson greens and blues of the iron bed.

Old Mr. Wycherley went to her and undid the small pearl buttons at her throat. He was very careful with her, unhooking her sleeves to the elbow, carefully, as if her bones were made of glass, lifting her skirt to loosen her garters, his fingers quivering with age. When he laid the lace collar back from her neck, the whalebonings in their frenzy seemed to writhe. Only when he touched the quaking brim of her hat did she stir and say:

"Hold on, Mr. W., I'll keep my hat where it is."

Mr. Wycherley took off his own jacket, folded it, and set it down with his cane and his bowler hat on a chair. His white linen vest covered his braces from sight, but in a moment he took that off and laid it in a drawer with his black silk stock. She could see his face reflected in the glass, the fine-wrinkled jowls hanging, and the wild eyebrows standing forth, white and abundant. There was a strange, a powerful, smile of victory on his mouth.

"Life," he called out, "ah, life, ah, life, the tricks it can conceive to play on one! Inestimable, inestimable, and one must be prepared with a countercheck for every move that's made!"

So he spoke to the memory of his wife left lying on the bed, or to the ear that eavesdropped forever in censure. He doubled his arm up above the elbow. His arm was bony and long, and when he clenched the long, loose hand the shifting ball of muscle rolled up, anchored as it was by the full blue veins under his skin.

"You've got a husband, Mrs. W.," he said with his vanity getting the best of him at last. "A man to stand between you and the onslaught. Let me to it. There's a man's work to be done."

II

Mr. Wycherley made the tea at seven in the morning and bore it on a tray to the thin little old lady who sat motionless against the pillows. She was sitting quite erect, but her head, with the black lace hat still on it, was drooping forward like a heavy wilting flower. She had no human look in her eye for him; the canny, the wily jet of her eyesight ran here and there at random like shiny beads unstrung.

"When you've had your tea, then you'll dress and go, Mrs. W.," said old Mr. Wycherley, setting the tea down beside her. She was looking through him at the wood of their dark, ancient furniture beyond. Her glance clicked over the glass of the wardrobe that held so many beauties; it might have been a silver screen on which the great dramas of her youth and life were passing.

"There may be harsh words exchanged," Mr. Wycherley was saying, and he watched her hand fall in greed upon the bread by her plate. "I wouldn't want you to hear anything unpleasant, Mrs. W."

"Damned if I'll move a foot," said Mrs. Wycherley. Her eyes had bubbled up from the source of misery again and were turned upon his face. If it had come into her head that this was the first time they had spoken of separation, or had come to things and not passed through them together, she gave no sign of it. Mutely she took down her tea and stepped from the bed while Mr. Wycherley finished his dressing. It was the touch of the goat-hair hide under her bare foot that startled the memory in her. She stooped and seized it up by one corner, and the lace hat quivered in wild agitation on her head.

"Mr. W.," she said, "I'll take the goat rug with me."

When she was dressed in her velvet, she pinned the rug over her shoulders. She moved quietly down the hall, with an aura of dust riding out from behind, and through the parlor in silence. In front of the chimney piece she paused and vaguely plucked a candelabra from the mantelshelf. She went mutely, a ravaged, haggard-eyed queen of sorrow, mutely after Mr. Wycherley into the kitchen, with her plum skirt following elegantly behind. One hand was fast on the handle of her cane, and the candelabra was in the other. When she drifted to a halt at the stove, she saw that Mr. Wycherley was laughing. The laughter was shaking under his linen vest and blowing in dry blasts through his conqueror's nose.

He said: "I've done a most ingenious thing, Mrs. W." He pointed to the sink, and Mrs. Wycherley saw the string and the rubber hosing whipped fast around the faucet. "This runs through the hall," said her husband, "ties up with a sinker and fishing rod over the front door and carries the aqueduct upwards."

He offered her his arm, and they went down the length of the narrow sightless corridor together. It seemed a gay and lavish thing to Mrs. Wycherley, a thing in preparation for a fete, the cord and the hosing winding in and out like a clinging vine above them. Mr. Wycherley was laughing youthfully by her side. "If anyone pulls the bell handle," he said, "a stream of fresh water jerked through the transom will persuade our good friends to think twice before ringing again. . . ."

Slowly, as Mr. Wycherley explained, Mrs. Wycherley began to see it; slowly, revealingly, like a negative emerging, shadow by shadow, from its acid bath. The two old people stood there laughing, their loose jaws fallen open, their limbs shaking with their clamor, snickering in their skins, and their necks stretched for it.

"Once you are safely out, Mrs. W.," said Mr. Wycherley, suddenly clapping into silence his laughter, "I'll fetch the sack of flour on to the doorknob and raise it to the transom. . . ."

When Mrs. Wycherley stepped into the street, the freshness of his lips where he had saluted her was still cool as mint on the back of her hand.

"So he worked all night at that, did he?" said Mr. Jefferson. There he sat at the café table, harking to her under the deepening tides of sun.

But Mrs. Wycherley could not remember. She was sitting as if at ease with the American, with the goat rug fastened with nursery pins across her shoulders, but her face was pure of color, and blue pits of drama and fear were excavated under her bird-bright eyes.

"Perhaps half the week!" she said with spirit. "He's very ingenious, Mr. Jefferson!"

To this man, this absolute stranger, Mrs. Wycherley knew she had said many things. The evil empty glass of port was standing before her in the sun, and she felt its madness in her face: two coals of color burning as if the fever of her fear had smoldered into light.

"But it couldn't have been all the week," said Mr. Jefferson, patiently feeling the way.

"All I know," said Mrs. Wycherley with sudden conviction, "is that when he called my attention to it this morning, damned if I could believe my eyes!"

"Ho, ho, an inventor!" said Mr. Jefferson slowly. "By George, it takes the old guys! Look at Edison. Thomas Edison."

"I don't know who he is," said Mrs. Wycherley, facing him with her hard, sharp, unchanging eyes.

"Well, take Bell," said Mr. Jefferson. "Take Bell . . ."

"Take Mr. Wycherley, damn it," said the old lady sharply. "Eleven o'clock now, and no sign of him." She gave her withered, wincing laugh and looked up slyly and sideways at Mr. Jefferson. "If he had the money to go on with his inventions, he might invent almost anything. He might invent the wireless if he were given any support."

"Yes, it takes his kind of mind to think of such things," said Mr. Jefferson, shaking his head. "Like that flour-and-water invention," he said, trotting his tongue, lost in thought or awe on the other side of the table.

When Mrs. Wycherley stood up, the promenade swept about and made a deep curtsy to her. She put out her hand and lifted the candelabra from the café table and held it forth.

"Mr. Jefferson, I am beginning to feel perturbed about Mr. W.," she said, and the words were strange and cumbrous on her tongue.

"I'll walk along with you, ma'am, if you'll allow," said Mr. Jefferson, rising.

She knew she was in a state of intoxication when she tried to climb the stairs.

"We were expecting unpleasant callers this morning, Mr. Jefferson," she said brightly, and suddenly she put her hand to the side of her face and began to cry.

"Why, Mrs. Wycherley," said the American, taking the candelabra from her, "this is too bad, now, too bad."

"It was the police who were coming," she said, but the sound of the truth was as good as a slap in the face to her. She looked straight into Mr. Jefferson's blue eyes; standing there fierce and straight, with her hand quivering on her cane.

"They're persecuting him because he's a genius, Mr.

Jefferson," she said fiercely. "They've accused him of plagiarism. But it is isn't so. He was the first, the very first, but they're after him for being clever."

"The police!" said Mr. Jefferson. He whistled softly. "You don't say so, Mrs. Wycherley!"

They started up the stairs, Mr. Jefferson's arm on one side of her, and the cane on the other to bear her up, and the empty candelabra held in Mr. Jefferson's hand.

"The police are all from Corsica here," Mrs. Wycherley was saying wildly. "If they see anyone with force of character, they must track them down. They've been waiting year after year for another leader. They're so envious of the Italians because of Mussolini, whose name we mustn't say here. You must call him Mr. Smith, Mr. Jefferson, whenever you speak of him. Mr. W. keeps me up on politics. If they've put him in jail, I'll get in touch with someone higher up. Anatole France said if there was ever any trouble we were to let him know."

The breath was shaking for peace in her throat, and at the fourth-floor landing they halted. There was flour and water spilled out on the boards there, and the blue warning was pasted still on the door.

"If Mr. W. had the wherewithal," said the old lady hoarsely, "damned if they'd attack him."

When she lifted her quivering hand and drew the long pin from the lacy crown, her hat went riding sideways on her head. Mr. Jefferson stood by, watching her as she ran the pin under the notice, ripping it up in soft furrows of paper with the flexible length of the pin. Her mouth was drawn up and tied fast like a bowknot under her nose, and her eyes never shed their inscrutable dark veneer. But Mr. Jefferson did not believe in what he saw; old ladies, their hair, their frailty, their querulousness even, struck a chord of puerile gallantry in his heart.

Mrs. Wycherley pulled the rope of the hanging bell and

a jet of water sprang out from the transom and fell upon
their heads. There they stood quietly waiting, Mrs. Wycherley under the goat-skin rug, and the water dripping quietly
off the brim of Mr. Jefferson's Panama hat and down the
length of his nose; the candelabra in Mr. Jefferson's hand
held to the fore, as if to cast light on the landing's darkness.

After a while, Mrs. Wycherley called out: "Benedict!
Benedict!" She rapped on the panel of the door with the
head of her delicate cane, and they heard the bolts slip on
the other side, and then Mr. Wycherley opened the door
slightly.

"Mr. Wycherley," the American began at once, "I've been
hearing a great deal about your inventions."

They could see him, wedged, tall and overbearing, sus-
picious still, in the opening, with his yellowish hair parted
like wax on his head; uncertain, and fingering the chain on
his vest, not quite ready to open to them.

"You're very kind indeed, sir," said Mr. Wycherley, bowing. "Won't you and your wife step inside?"

"My wife?" said Mr. Jefferson, but there was no confusion in the old lady's face. She put her arm through the
American's. "This is Mrs. Wycherley!" Mr. Jefferson said.

The old man opened the door to them.

"Ah, yes, I dare say it is," he said wearily. Wearily he
led the way into the parlor and indicated the armchairs in
the shadow to them. His shoulders, in the great length of
his coat, were stooped; even his presence, so schooled, so
rigid, seemed drooping on the air. "I haven't seen her for
some years," he said.

Mr. Jefferson set the candelabra on the mantelpiece, and
Mrs. Wycherley unpinned the goatskin rug from her shoulders and spread it on the floor. When they were seated, the
three of them in the dimness of the blinded room, Mr.
Jefferson began to speak.

"I'm interested in inventions," he said with respect. "I think I could make it worth your while to go on, Mr. Wycherley."

The old lady lifted her hand to remove the remaining pins from her hat and looked sharply at the American.

"I'd like to donate some money," said Mr. Jefferson, "to the interests of science."

"My good sir," said Mr. Wycherley with his aged, withering charm, "you are very kind, but I could not hear of it."

Mr. Jefferson turned his head and looked at the old lady, and Mrs. Wycherley looked sharply at the American and slowly winked one eye.

"My good sir," said Mr. Wycherley again, "if you are determined to persist upon the realization of inestimably high qualities, it is scarcely my place to forbid you to convert them into whatever exchange you value. But I must say that I consider it an act in very questionable taste, and I insist that it be regarded in the light of a temporary loan."

In the mock twilight of the shuttered room, the three of them sat waiting for what next would be said.

"I could arrange to pay you a percentage," said Mr. Wycherley in a measured tone out of the stillness.

"Yes," said Mr. Jefferson. "That would do very well. A percentage on every invention made."

A week later Mr. Jefferson went back to the States, and they never saw anything more of him except the money and the postcards he sent.

III

It was the second year after the money began coming to them that Mrs. Wycherley brought the first cats in from the street. Whether they would or whether they wouldn't, she would have them in off the street and into the back room next the kitchen: the men of the race to the one side with a barricade of chicken wire between them and the mothers and young on the other.

She would go over the back fences of the quarter for them, for now that Mr. Wycherley was an inventor, a man who went his own way, his time was taken up and his hours filled for him. When Mrs. Wycherley came in on tiptoe with her latest cat under her arm, she could see him sitting in the parlor, his hands folded on the papers that she had laid neatly on the table before him. The cries of the newest cat caught and held fast in her hands pierced the absolute silence of what Mr. Wycherley was always about to do.

It was as if their status had been altered, for the time was no longer left to them to linger on the promenade at the café tables, speaking with people there they knew. Twice in the week they went out together, but now Mr. Wycherley was a man with a vision, an inventor, and the menace of his career hung over them like a shadow about to fall.

In December the neighbors began speaking of it, began saying that Mr. Wycherley did not come out any more. They spoke to the old lady in the hall, and then they passed on, wondering. The look on her face was strange and high and secret. Only once, when the two women were shaking out their door mats at their thresholds, did the neighbor opposite on the landing speak to Mrs. Wycherley about her husband.

"How is Mr. Wycherley these days?" the Frenchwoman said.

The wave of pride and secrecy went over the old lady's delicate crumpled face, rose to the smooth edifice of her brow, submerged feature after feature until only her clear obdurate eyes were left exempt.

"Mr. Wycherley is absorbed in his inventing," she said. She spoke with such equity, such natural contempt, that it put an end at once to the questioning. In a moment she stooped over and shook out the mat in her brittle hand.

There was a mauve silk scarf tied around her head to save her hair from dust.

"It is something that will keep flowers from fading," she said to the other woman. The two of them looked strangely at each other across the dusty landing. "It is something to keep the dead from corruption," said Mrs. Wycherley with an evil gleam. "It will make him famous all over the world."

The neighbor watched her drift through her own doorway, move like a sleepwalker into the dark of her own corridor. There was no other word spoken, no sound except the whisper of the old lady's slippers over the tiles, slipping, slipping into the absolute darkness, and then the door closed behind.

In this way they saw her sliding out all through the month of December, moving out as if in a dream to fetch the bread on the Place Garibaldi and the other things the two of them were used to eat. But when on New Year's Eve there was no sign of Mr. Wycherley, then the story began to run from mouth to mouth throughout the house. They began to say that Mr. Wycherley had taken the money out of the bank and run away from his wife. They all knew about the money the rich American had given, and they began saying that it was the number of cats in the apartment that had driven Mr. Wycherley mad. He must have taken his clothes and things with him at night and gone off early in December; a month now since he had gone away.

The story was blowing like a high wind through the place, so after the holidays the proprietor came and asked for Mr. Wycherley. It was the middle of the morning, and Mrs. Wycherley was dressed for her shopping, with her lace collar buttoned up under her ears. There she stood in the piece of the doorway, her hat on, peering up her nose, looking, as if sightless, up into the proprietor's thick, unflickering face. Everyone had a certain respect and homage for this man, and now special concern because his son, an automobile racer, had been killed on the race course in his Bugatti scarcely a week before.

The bereaved father stood at the door dressed in his clothes of mourning. There was a hush and expectancy up and down the halls and stairways of the house. He was dressed in black for the death of his son, but because he was a Niçois there was much of the Italian in him, and behind his solemn mask and sleeping temper there was almost a chuckle waiting in his throat. He took off his broad black hat and spoke gravely to Mrs. Wycherley.

"I'd like to have a word or two with your husband, with Mr. Wycherley," he said.

"Mr. Wycherley is busy with his work," said the old lady, but even as she spoke her spirit faltered and swooned. She was too weary, too old, too worn now to face them alone. She shrank back against the wall and the man pushed his own way in. He went down the dark passage, clearing his throat aloud, attempting to hum a tune in his throat to hearten his dismay. Now he knew, now he knew what it was for certain. He beat his broad black hat against the side of his trousers as he walked. Now he knew, he knew very well. He knew what he was going to see when he opened the parlor door. He took out his handkerchief and covered his nose and mouth with it before he walked into the room.

Mr. Wycherley was sitting fully dressed at the table, but he made no move when the proprietor came in. His hands were laid out on the papers before him and his head had fallen sideways. The old lady came up and stood still in the doorway.

"You see, he's working," she said.

"Yes," said the proprietor, "yes, I see."

He went out into the hall with her and closed the door, and he said: "I'll be back in a little while, Mrs. Wycherley. We'll have to take your husband away."

"No, he'll stay here, damn it," said the old lady sharply. "I won't let him out of the house in the delicate condition he's in."

"We aren't going to hurt him," said the proprietor, putting his hat on. "I'll come back with some friends and we'll take him out for a little drive."

He was not afraid, he had seen death before, and in violent shapes and ways he had seen it. But he wanted to get quickly down the hall and out of the door. He shook Mrs. Wycherley's breakable hand, and he said:

"A little air won't harm him, Mrs. Wycherley."

She could hear the chuckle lurking in his throat.

"Mr. W.," she said vaguely at the door, "he never cared for driving. You're very kind, I'm sure."

The report ran this way: it said that when the door was broken in there was nothing to be seen in the darkness, but the objects, whatever they were, hanging over the door hit every officer in the face as he passed under. Once they switched on the light they saw it was the old English lady hanging, hung just there in the doorway, with malice, so that her feet caught each one of them, even the proprietor, square in the face as he passed.

And that was not the end of it. After they cut her down and found she was dead, then the cats began running wild from the doors they opened in the back rooms of the apartment. The gendarmes, the short Corsican men, had their clubs in their hands and struck them down like rats. There were over a hundred cats, it was said, flying like demons at the faces of the officers, and the back rooms foul with them. Mr. Jefferson read this in Ohio, but even then he did not believe the truth; he never for a minute saw them as a grasping, sinister old pair.

A WHITE HERON

By Sarah Orne Jewett

The woods were already filled with shadows one June evening, just before eight o'clock, though a bright sunset still glimmered faintly among the trunks of the trees. A little girl was driving home her cow, a plodding, dilatory, provoking creature in her behavior, but a valued companion for all that. They were going away from whatever light there was, and striking deep into the woods, but their feet were familiar with the path, and it was no matter whether their eyes could see it or not.

There was hardly a night the summer through when the old cow could be found waiting at the pasture bars; on the contrary, it was her greatest pleasure to hide herself away among the huckleberry bushes, and though she wore a loud bell she had made the discovery that if one stood perfectly still it would not ring. So Sylvia had to hunt for her until she found her, and call Co'! Co'! with never an answering Moo, until her childish patience was quite spent. If the creature had not given good milk and plenty of it, the case would have seemed very different to her owners. Besides, Sylvia had all the time there was, and very little use to make of it. Sometimes in pleasant weather it was a consolation to look upon the cow's pranks as an intelligent attempt to play hide and seek, and as the child had no playmates she lent herself to this amusement with a good deal of zest. Though this chase had been so long that the wary animal herself had given an unusual signal of her whereabouts, Sylvia had only laughed when she came upon Mistress Moolly at the swampside, and urged her affectionately homeward with a twig of birch leaves. The old cow was not inclined to wander farther, she even turned in the right direction for once as they left the pasture, and stepped along the road at a good pace. She was quite ready to be milked now, and seldom stopped to browse. Sylvia wondered what her grandmother would say because they were so late. It was a great while since she had left home at half-past five o'clock, but everybody knew the difficulty of making this errand a short one. Mrs. Tilley had chased the hornéd torment too many summer evenings herself to blame any one else for lingering, and was only thankful as she waited that she had Sylvia, nowadays, to give such valuable assistance. The good woman suspected that Sylvia loitered occasionally on her own account; there never was such a child for straying about out-of-doors since the world was made! Everybody said that it was a good change for a little maid who had tried to grow for eight years in a crowded manufacturing town, but, as for Sylvia herself, it seemed as if she never had been alive at all before she came to live at the farm. She thought often with wistful compassion of a wretched geranium that belonged to a town neighbor.

" 'Afraid of folks,' " old Mrs. Tilley said to herself, with a smile, after she had made the unlikely choice of Sylvia from her daughter's houseful of children, and was returning to the farm. " 'Afraid of folks,' they said! I guess she won't be troubled no great with 'em up to the old place!" When they reached the door of the lonely house and stopped to unlock it, and the cat came to purr loudly, and rub against them, a deserted pussy, indeed, but fat with young robins, Sylvia whispered that this was a beautiful place to live in, and she never should wish to go home.

The companions followed the shady wood-road, the cow taking slow steps and the child very fast ones. The cow stopped long at the brook to drink, as if the pasture were not half a swamp, and Sylvia stood still and waited, letting her bare feet cool themselves in the shoal water, while the great twilight moths struck softly against her. She waded on through the brook as the cow moved away, and listened to the thrushes with a heart that beat fast with pleasure. There was a stirring in the great boughs overhead. They were full of little birds and beasts that seemed to be wide awake, and going about their world, or else saying good-night to each other in sleepy twitters. Sylvia herself felt sleepy as she walked along. However, it was not much farther to the house, and the air was soft and sweet. She was not often in the woods so late as this, and it made her feel as if she were a part of the gray shadows and the moving leaves. She was just thinking how long it seemed since she first came to the farm a year ago, and wondering if everything went on in the noisy town just the same as when she was there; the thought of the great red-faced boy who used to chase and frighten her made her hurry along the path to escape from the shadow of the trees.

Suddenly this little woods-girl is horror-stricken to hear a clear whistle not very far away. Not a bird's-whistle, which would have a sort of friendliness, but a boy's whistle, determined, and somewhat aggressive. Sylvia left the cow to whatever sad fate might await her, and stepped discreetly aside into the bushes, but she was just too late. The enemy had discovered her, and called out in a very cheerful and persuasive tone, "Halloa, little girl, how far is it to the road?" and trembling Sylvia answered almost inaudibly, "A good ways."

She did not dare to look boldly at the tall young man, who carried a gun over his shoulder, but she came out of her bush and again followed the cow, while he walked alongside.

"I have been hunting for some birds," the stranger said kindly, "and I have lost my way, and need a friend very much. Don't be afraid," he added gallantly. "Speak up and tell me what your name is, and whether you think I can spend the night at your house, and go out gunning early in the morning."

Sylvia was more alarmed than before. Would not her grandmother consider her much to blame? But who could have foreseen such an accident as this? It did not seem to be her fault, and she hung her head as if the stem of it were broken, but managed to answer "Sylvy," with much effort when her companion again asked her name.

Mrs. Tilley was standing in the doorway when the trio came into view. The cow gave a loud moo by way of explanation.

"Yes, you'd better speak up for yourself, you old trial! Where'd she tucked herself away this time, Sylvy?" But Sylvia kept an awed silence; she knew by instinct that her grandmother did not comprehend the gravity of the situation. She must be mistaking the stranger for one of the farmer-lads of the region.

The young man stood his gun beside the door, and dropped a lumpy game-bag beside it; then he bade Mrs. Tilley good-evening, and repeated his wayfarer's story, and asked if he could have a night's lodging.

"Put me anywhere you like," he said. "I must be off early in the morning, before day; but I am very hungry, indeed. You can give me some milk at any rate, that's plain."

"Dear sakes, yes," responded the hostess, whose long slumbering hospitality seemed to be easily awakened. "You might fare better if you went out to the main road a mile

or so, but you're welcome to what we've got. I'll milk right
off, and you make yourself at home. You can sleep on husks
or feathers," she proffered graciously. "I raised them all
myself. There's good pasturing for geese just below here
towards the ma'sh. Now step round and set a plate for the
gentleman, Sylvy!" And Sylvia promptly stepped. She was
glad to have something to do, and she was hungry herself.

It was a surprise to find so clean and comfortable a little
dwelling in this New England wilderness. The young man
had known the horrors of its most primitive housekeeping,
and the dreary squalor of that level of society which does
not rebel at the companionship of hens. This was the best
thrift of an old-fashioned farmstead, though on such a small
scale that it seemed like a hermitage. He listened eagerly
to the old woman's quaint talk, he watched Sylvia's pale
face and shining gray eyes with ever growing enthusiasm,
and insisted that this was the best supper he had eaten for
a month, and afterward the new-made friends sat down in
the door-way together while the moon came up.

Soon it would be berry-time, and Sylvia was a great help
at picking. The cow was a good milker, though a plaguy
thing to keep track of, the hostess gossiped frankly, adding
presently that she had buried four children, so Sylvia's
mother, and a son (who might be dead) in California were
all the children she had left. "Dan, my boy, was a great hand
to go gunning," she explained sadly. "I never wanted for
pa'tridges or gray squer'ls while he was to home. He's been
a great wand'rer, I expect, and he's no hand to write letters.
There, I don't blame him, I'd ha' seen the world myself if
it had been so I could."

"Sylvy takes after him," the grandmother continued affectionately, after a minute's pause. "There ain't a foot o'
ground she don't know her way over, and the wild creaturs
counts her one o' themselves. Squer'ls she'll tame to come

an' feed right out o' her hands, and all sorts o' birds. Last winter she got the jay-birds to bangeing here, and I believe she'd 'a' scanted herself of her own meals to have plenty to throw out amongst 'em, if I had n't kep' watch. Anything but crows, I tell her, I'm willin' to help support — though Dan he had a tamed one o' them that did seem to have reason same as folks. It was round here a good spell after he went away. Dan an' his father they did n't hitch, — but he never held up his head ag'in after Dan had dared him an' gone off."

The guest did not notice this hint of family sorrows in his eager interest in something else.

"So Sylvy knows all about birds, does she?" he exclaimed, as he looked round at the little girl who sat, very demure but increasingly sleepy, in the moonlight. "I am making a collection of birds myself. I have been at it ever since I was a boy." (Mrs. Tilley smiled.) "There are two or three very rare ones I have been hunting for these five years. I mean to get them on my own ground if they can be found."

"Do you cage 'em up?" asked Mrs. Tilley doubtfully, in response to this enthusiastic announcement.

"Oh no, they're stuffed and preserved, dozens and dozens of them," said the ornithologist, "and I have shot or snared every one myself. I caught a glimpse of a white heron a few miles from here on Saturday, and I have followed it in this direction. They have never been found in this district at all. The little white heron, it is," and he turned again to look at Sylvia with the hope of discovering that the rare bird was one of her acquaintances.

But Sylvia was watching a hop-toad in the narrow footpath.

"You would know the heron if you saw it," the stranger continued eagerly. "A queer tall white bird with soft feathers and long thin legs. And it would have a nest perhaps in the top of a high tree, made of sticks, something like a hawk's nest."

Sylvia's heart gave a wild beat; she knew that strange white bird, and had once stolen softly near where it stood in some bright green swamp grass, away over at the other side of the woods. There was an open place where the sunshine always seemed strangely yellow and hot, where tall, nodding rushes grew, and her grandmother had warned her that she might sink in the soft black mud underneath and never be heard of more. Not far beyond were the salt marshes just this side the sea itself, which Sylvia wondered and dreamed much about, but never had seen, whose great voice could sometimes be heard above the noise of the woods on stormy nights.

"I can't think of anything I should like so much as to find that heron's nest," the handsome stranger was saying. "I would give ten dollars to anybody who could show it to me," he added desperately, "and I mean to spend my whole vacation hunting for it if need be. Perhaps it was only migrating, or had been chased out of its own region by some bird of prey."

Mrs. Tilley gave amazed attention to all this, but Sylvia still watched the toad, not divining, as she might have done at some calmer time, that the creature wished to get to its hole under the door-step, and was much hindered by the unusual spectators at that hour of the evening. No amount of thought, that night, could decide how many wished-for treasures the ten dollars, so lightly spoken of, would buy.

The next day the young sportsman hovered about the woods, and Sylvia kept him company, having lost her first fear of the friendly lad, who proved to be most kind and sympathetic. He told her many things about the birds and what they knew and where they lived and what they did with themselves. And he gave her a jackknife, which she thought as great a treasure as if she were a desert-islander. All day long he did not once make her troubled or afraid except when he brought down some unsuspecting singing creature from its bough. Sylvia would have liked him vastly better without his gun; she could not understand why he killed the very birds he seemed to like so much. But as the day waned, Sylvia still watched the young man with loving admiration. She had never seen anybody so charming and delightful; the woman's heart, asleep in the child, was vaguely thrilled by a dream of love. Some premonition of that great power stirred and swayed these young creatures who traversed the solemn woodlands with soft-footed silent care. They stopped to listen to a bird's song; they pressed forward again eagerly, parting the branches — speaking to each other rarely and in whispers; the young man going first and Sylvia following, fascinated, a few steps behind, with her gray eyes dark with excitement.

She grieved because the longed-for white heron was elusive, but she did not lead the guest, she only followed, and there was no such thing as speaking first. The sound of her own unquestioned voice would have terrified her — it was hard enough to answer yes or no when there was need of that. At last evening began to fall, and they drove the cow home together, and Sylvia smiled with pleasure when they came to the place where she heard the whistle and was afraid only the night before.

II

Half a mile from home, at the farther edge of the woods, where the land was highest, a great pine-tree stood, the last of its generation. Whether it was left for a boundary mark, or for what reason, no one could say; the wood-choppers who had felled its mates were dead and gone long ago, and a whole forest of sturdy trees, pines and oaks and maples, had grown again. But the stately head of this old pine towered above them all and made a landmark for sea and shore miles and miles away. Sylvia knew it well. She had always believed that whoever climbed to the top of it could see the ocean; and the little girl had often laid her hand on the great rough trunk and looked up wistfully at those dark boughs that the wind always stirred, no matter how hot and still the air might be below. Now she thought of the tree with a new excitement, for why, if one climbed it at break of day, could not one see all the world, and easily discover from whence the white heron flew, and mark the place, and find the hidden nest?

What a spirit of adventure, what wild ambition! What fancied triumph and delight and glory for the later morning when she could make known the secret! It was almost too real and too great for the childish heart to bear.

All night the door of the little house stood open and the whippoorwills came and sang upon the very step. The young sportsman and his old hostess were sound asleep, but Sylvia's great design kept her broad awake and watching. She forgot to think of sleep. The short summer night seemed as long as the winter darkness, and at last when the whippoorwills ceased, and she was afraid the morning would after all come too soon, she stole out of the house and followed the pasture path through the woods, hastening toward the open ground beyond, listening with a sense of comfort and companionship to the drowsy twitter of a half-awakened bird, whose perch she had jarred in passing. Alas, if the great wave of human interest which flooded for the first time this dull little life should sweep away the satisfactions of an existence heart to heart with nature and the dumb life of the forest!

There was the huge tree asleep yet in the paling moonlight, and small and silly Sylvia began with utmost bravery to mount to the top of it, with tingling, eager blood coursing the channels of her whole frame, with her bare feet and fingers, that pinched and held like bird's claws to the monstrous ladder reaching up, up, almost to the sky itself. First she must mount the white oak tree that grew alongside, where she was almost lost among the dark branches and the green leaves heavy and wet with dew; a bird fluttered off its nest, and a red squirrel ran to and fro and scolded pettishly at the harmless housebreaker. Sylvia felt her way easily. She had often climbed there, and knew that higher still one of the oak's upper branches chafed against the pine trunk, just where its lower boughs were set close together. There, when she made the dangerous pass from one tree to the other, the great enterprise would really begin.

She crept out along the swaying oak limb at last, and took the daring step across into the old pine-tree. The way was harder than she thought; she must reach far and hold fast, the sharp dry twigs caught and held her and scratched her like angry talons, the pitch made her thin little fingers clumsy and stiff as she went round and round the tree's great stem, higher and higher upward. The sparrows and robins in the woods below were beginning to wake and twitter to the dawn, yet it seemed much lighter there aloft in the pine-tree, and the child knew she must hurry if her project were to be of any use.

The tree seemed to lengthen itself out as she went up, and to reach farther and farther upward. It was like a great mainmast to the voyaging earth; it must truly have been amazed that morning through all its ponderous frame as it felt this determined spark of human spirit wending its way from higher branch to branch. Who knows how steadily the least twigs held themselves to advantage this light, weak creature on her way! The old pine must have loved his new dependent. More than all the hawks, and bats, and moths, and even the sweet voiced thrushes, was the brave, beating heart of the solitary gray-eyed child. And the tree stood still and frowned away the winds that June morning while the dawn grew bright in the east.

Sylvia's face was like a pale star, if one had seen it from the ground, when the last thorny bough was past, and she stood trembling and tired but wholly triumphant, high in the tree-top. Yes, there was the sea with the dawning sun making a golden dazzle over it, and toward that glorious east flew two hawks with slow-moving pinions. How low they looked in the air from that height when one had only seen them before far up, and dark against the blue sky. Their gray feathers were as soft as moths; they seemed only a little way from the tree, and Sylvia felt as if she too could go flying away among the clouds. Westward, the woodlands and farms reached miles and miles into the distance; here and there were church steeples, and white villages, truly it was a vast and awesome world!

The birds sang louder and louder. At last the sun came up bewilderingly bright. Sylvia could see the white sails of ships out at sea, and the clouds that were purple and rose-colored and yellow at first began to fade away. Where was the white heron's nest in the sea of green branches, and was this wonderful sight and pageant of the world the only reward for having climbed to such a giddy height? Now look down again, Sylvia, where the green marsh is set among the shining birches and dark hemlocks; there where you saw the white heron once you will see him again; look, look! a white spot of him like a single floating feather comes up from the dead hemlock and grows larger, and rises, and comes close at last, and goes by the landmark pine with steady sweep of wing and outstretched slender neck and crested head. And wait! wait! do not move a foot or a finger, little girl, do not send an arrow of light and consciousness from your two eager eyes, for the heron has perched on a pine bough

not far beyond yours, and cries back to his mate on the nest
and plumes his feathers for the new day!

The child gives a long sigh a minute later when a company of shouting cat-birds comes also to the tree, and vexed
by their fluttering and lawlessness the solemn heron goes
away. She knows his secret now, the wild, light, slender bird
that floats and wavers, and goes back like an arrow presently
to his home in the green world beneath. Then Sylvia, well
satisfied, makes her perilous way down again, not daring to
look far below the branch she stands on, ready to cry sometimes because her fingers ache and her lamed feet slip.
Wondering over and over again what the stranger would
say to her, and what he would think when she told him how
to find his way straight to the heron's nest.

"Sylvy, Sylvy!" called the busy old grandmother again
and again, but nobody answered, and the small husk bed
was empty and Sylvia had disappeared.

The guest waked from a dream, and remembering his
day's pleasure hurried to dress himself that might it sooner
begin. He was sure from the way the shy little girl looked
once or twice yesterday that she had at least seen the white
heron, and now she must really be made to tell. Here she
comes now, paler than ever, and her worn old frock is torn
and tattered, and smeared with pine pitch. The grandmother
and the sportsman stand in the door together and question
her, and the splendid moment has come to speak of the dead
hemlock-tree by the green marsh.

But Sylvia does not speak after all, though the old grandmother fretfully rebukes her, and the young man's kind,
appealing eyes are looking straight in her own. He can make
them rich with money; he has promised it, and they are poor
now. He is so well worth making happy, and he waits to
hear the story she can tell.

No, she must keep silence! What is it that suddenly forbids her and makes her dumb? Has she been nine years growing and now, when the great world for the first time puts out a hand to her, must she thrust it aside for a bird's sake? The murmur of the pine's green branches is in her ears, she remembers how the white heron came flying through the golden air and how they watched the sea and the morning together, and Sylvia cannot speak; she cannot tell the heron's secret and give its life away.

Dear loyalty, that suffered a sharp pang as the guest went away disappointed later in the day, that could have served and followed him and loved him as a dog loves! Many a night Sylvia heard the echo of his whistle haunting the pasture path as she came home with the loitering cow. She forgot even her sorrow at the sharp report of his gun and the sight of thrushes and sparrows dropping silent to the ground, their songs hushed and their pretty feathers stained and wet with blood. Were the birds better friends than their hunter might have been, — who can tell? Whatever treasures were lost to her, woodlands and summer-time, remember! Bring your gifts and graces and tell your secrets to this lonely country child!

THE RAID

By Alun Lewis

My platoon and I were on training that morning. We've been on training every morning for the last three years, for that matter. On this occasion it was Current Affairs, which always boils down to how long the war is going to last, and when the orderly told me the C. O. wanted me in his office I broke the lads off for a cup of tea from the charwallah and nipped over to the orderly room, tidying myself· as I went. I didn't expect anything unusual until I took a cautionary peep through the straw window of his matting shed and saw a strange officer in there. So I did a real dapper salute and braced myself. Self-defence is always the first instinct, self-suspicion the second. But I hadn't been drunk since I came to India and I hadn't written anything except love in my letters. As for politics, as far as they're concerned I don't exist, I'm never in. The other chap was a major and had a red armband.

"Come in, Selden," the colonel said. "This is the D. A. P. M. Head of military police. Got a job for you. Got your map case?"

"No sir. It's in company office."

"Hurry off and fetch it."

When I came back they were hard at it, bending over the

inch map. The C. O. looked up. His face got very red when
he bent.

"Here's your objective, Selden. This village here, Chaudanullah. Eighteen miles away. Route: track south of Morje,
river-bed up to Pimpardi, turn south a mile before Pimpardi
and strike across the watershed on a fixed bearing. Work it
out with a protractor on the map and set your compass
before you march off. Strike the secondary road below this
group of huts here, 247568, cross the road and work up the
canal to the village. Throw a cordon round the village with
two sections of your platoon. Take the third yourself and
search the houses methodically. Government has a paid
agent in the village who will meet you at this canal bridge
here — got it? — at 06.00 hours. The agent reported that
your man arrived there last night after dark and is lying up
in one of the hovels."

"What man, sir?" I asked.

"Christ, didn't I tell you? Why the devil didn't you stop
me? This fellow, what's-his-name — it's all on that paper
there — he's wanted. Remember the bomb in the cinema last
Tuesday, killed three British other ranks? He's wanted for
that. Read the description before you go. Any questions so
far? Right. Well, you'll avoid all houses, make a detour
round villages, keep off the road all the way. Understand?
News travels faster than infantry in India. He'll be away
before you're within ten miles if you show yourself. Let's
see. Twenty miles by night. Give you ten hours. Leave here
at 19.30 hours. Arrive an hour before first light. Go in at
dawn, keep your eyes skinned. M. T. will R. V. outside the
village at dawn. Drive the prisoner straight to jail.
D. A. P. M. will be there."

"Very good, sir. Dress, sir?" I said.

"Dress? P.T. shoes, cloth caps, overalls, basic pouches,
rifles, 50 rounds of .303 per man, and grenades. 69 grenades

if he won't come out, 36 grenades if he makes a fight of it. Anything else?"

"No, sir."

"Good. Remember to avoid the villages. Stalk him good and proper. Keep up-wind of him. I'm picking you and your platoon because I think you're the best I've got. I want results, Selden."

"I'll give you a good show, sir."

"Bloody good shot with a point 22, Selden is," the C. O. said to the D. A. P. M. by way of light conversation. "Shot six mallard with me last Sunday."

"Of course we want the man alive, sir, if it's at all possible," the D. A. P. M. said, fiddling with his nervous pink moustache. "He's not proved guilty yet, you see, sir, and with public opinion in India what it is."

"Quite," said the colonel. "Quite. Make a note of that, Selden. Tell your men to shoot low."

"Very good, sir."

"Got the route marked on your talc?"

"Yes, sir." I'd marked the route in chinograph pencil and the Chaudanullah place in red as we do for enemy objectives. It was all thick.

"Rub it all off, then. Security. Read his description. Have you read it? What is it?"

"Dark eyes, sir. Scar on left knee. Prominent cheekbones. Left corner of mouth droops. Front incisor discoloured. Last seen wearing European suit, may be dressed in native dhoti, Mahratta style."

"And his ring?" said the C. O. He's as keen as mustard the old man is.

"Oh yes, sir. Plain gold wedding ring."

"Correct. Don't forget these details. Invaluable sometimes. Off with you."

I saluted and marched out.

"Damn good fellow, Selden," I heard the C. O. say. "Your man is in the bag."

I felt pretty pleased with that. Comes of shooting those six mallard.

The platoon was reassembling after their tea and I felt pretty important, going back with all that dope. After all, it was the first bit of action we'd seen in two and a half years. It would be good for morale. I knew they'd moan like hell, having to do a twenty-mile route march by night, but I could sell them that all right. So I fell them in in threes and called them to attention for disciplinary reasons and told them they'd been picked for a special job and this was it. . . .

They were very impressed by the time I'd finished.

"Any questions?" I said.

"Yes, sir," said Chalky White. He was an L. P. T. B. conductor and you won't find him forgetting a halfpenny. "Do we take haversack rations and will we be in time for breakfast?" He thinks the same way as Napoleon.

"Yes," I said. "Anything else?"

"What's this fellow done, sir?" Bottomley asked, then. Bottomley always was a bit Bolshie, and he's had his knife into me for two and a half years because I was a bank clerk in Civvy Street and played golf on Sundays.

"Killed three troops, I think," I said. "Is that good enough?"

I felt I'd scored pretty heavy over his Red stuff this time.

"Right," I said. "Break off till 19.00 hours. Keep your mouths shut. White will draw rations at the cookhouse. No cigarettes or matches will be taken."

I did that for disciplinary purposes. They didn't say a word. Pretty good.

We crossed the start line dead on 19.30 hours and everybody looked at us with some interest. I felt mighty "hush-

hush." My security was first class. Hadn't told a soul, except Ken More and Ted Paynter.

"Bring 'em back alive," a soldier jeered outside the cookhouse.

Somebody's let the cat out of the bag. Damn them all. Can't trust a soul in the ranks with the skin of a sausage.

Anyway, we got going bang away. I knew the first stretch past Morje and Pimpardi and we did about three miles an hour there. The night was breathless and stuffy; we put hankies round our foreheads to keep the sweat out of our eyes. And the perpetual buzzing of the crickets got on my nerves like a motor horn when the points jam and all the pedestrians laugh. I suppose I was a bit worked up. Every time a mosquito or midge touched me I let out a blow fit to knacker a bull. But I settled down after a while and began to enjoy the sense of freedom and deep still peace that informs the night out in the tropics. You've read all about tropical stars; well, it's quite true. They're marvellous; and we use some of them for direction-finding at night too. The Plough, for instance, and one called Cassiopeia that you bisect for the Pole Star.

Then there was the tricky bit over the mountain by compass. I just hoped for the best on that leg. Luckily the moon came up and put the lads in a good mood. I allowed them to talk in whispers for one hour and they had to keep silent for the next hour for disciplinary reasons. We halted for half an hour on the crest of the watershed and ate our bully beef sandwiches with relish, though bully tastes like a hot poultice out here. It was a damn fine view from that crest. A broad valley a thousand feet below with clusters of fires in the villages and round a hill temple on the other side. Either a festival or a funeral, obviously. I could hear the drums beating there, too; it was very clear and echoing, made my flesh creep. You feel so out of it in India somehow. You just slink around in the wilds and you feel very white and different. I don't know. . . . You know, I'd have said that valley *hated* us that night, on those rocky crests. Queer.

I didn't know which group of huts was which, but I could see the canal glittering in the moonlight so I was near enough right, praise be. The jackals were howling too, and some creature came right up to us, it gave me a scare. I knew that bully had a pretty bad stench. Anyway we got on the move again, Chalky White saying next stop Hammersmiff Bridge, and we slithered down as quietly as we could, hanging on to each other's rifles on the steep bits. We made our way between the villages and the drums beat themselves into a frenzy that had something personal about it. Then we went up the canal for about four miles, keeping about a hundred yards off the path and pretty rough going it was. Then we came to what I felt must be our objective, a cluster of crumbled huts on the foothills, pretty poor show even for these parts, and the boys were blistered and beat so I scattered them under the bushes and told them to lie low. It was only 5.30 a.m. and the agent fellow wasn't due until six. I had a nap myself, matter of fact, though it's a shootable offence. I woke up with a start and it was five past six, and I peered round my tree and there wasn't a sound. No drums, no jackals, no pie dogs. It was singing in my ears, the silence, and I wished to God we'd got this job over. It could go wrong so easily. He might fight, or his pals might help him, or he might have got wind of us, or I might have come to the wrong place. I was like an old woman. I loaded my Colt and felt better. Then I went down the canal to look for the chowkey fellow. I took a pretty poor view of a traitor, but I took a poorer view of him not turning up. He wasn't there and I walked up the path and just when

I was getting really scared he appeared out of nowhere
and I damn near shot him on the spot.

"Officer sahib huzzoor," he said. "Mai Sarkar ko dost hai,"
something. And he said the name of the man I was after,
which was the password.

"Achiba," I said, meaning good show. "Tairo a minute
while I bolo my phaltan and then we'll jao jillo." He got the
idea.

I nipped back and roused the lads quietly from under the
trees and we moved up like ghosts on that village. I never
want to see that village again. It was so still and fragile in
the reluctant grey light. Even the pie dogs were asleep, and
the bullocks lying on their sides. Once I travelled overnight
from Dieppe to Paris and the countryside looked just as
ghostly that morning. But this time it was dangerous. I had
a feeling somebody was going to die and there'd be a hell
of a shemozzle. And at the same time the houses looked so
poor and harmless, almost timid somehow. And the chowkey bloke was like a ghost. It was seeing him so scared that
put me steady again. He was afraid of being seen with us
as far as I could make out, and said he'd show us where this
fellow was lying up and then he'd disappear please. I said
never mind about the peace, let's get the war over first, and
I told Bottomley to watch the bloke in case he had anything
up his sleeve.

We got to the ring of trees outside the village without a
sound, and the two section leaders led their men round each
side of the village in a pincer movement. All the boys were
white and dirty and their eyes were like stones. I remember
suddenly feeling very proud of them just then.

I gave them ten minutes to get into position and close the
road at the rear of the village. And then a damned pie dog
set up a yelp over on the right flank and another replied with

a long shivering howl. I knew things would start going wrong if I didn't act quickly. We didn't want the village to find out until we'd gone if possible. For political reasons. And for reasons of health, I thought. So I gave the Follow-me sign and closed in on the huddled houses. There were a couple of outlying houses with a little shrine, and then the village proper with a crooked street running down it. The chowkey seemed to know where to go. I pointed to the single buildings and he said, "Nay, sahib," and pointed to the street. So I posted a man to picket the shrine and led the rest through the bush behind our scruffy guide. He moved like a beaten dog, crouching and limping, bare-foot. There was a dead ox in the bush and a pair of kites sleeping and gorged beside it. It stank like a bad death. Turned me. We hurried on. The bushes were in flower, sort of wisteria, the blossoms closed and drooping. We crept along under a tumbledown wall and paused, kneeling, at the street corner. I posted two men there, one on each side with fixed bayo-nets, to fire down the street if he bolted. The other two sec-tions would be covering it from the other end. Then I nudged the chowkey man and signalled to my grenade man and rifleman to cover me in. I slipped round the corner and went gingerly down the street. Suddenly I feel quite cool and excited at the same time. The chowkey went about fifteen yards down the street and then slunk against the wall on his knees, pointing inwards to the house he was kneeling against. It was made of branches woven with straw and reed, a beggared place. He looked up at me and my revolver and he was sweating with fear. He had the pox all over his face, too. I took a breath to steady myself, took the first pressure on my trigger, kicked the door lattice aside and jumped in. Stand in the light in the doorway and you're a dead man.

I crouched in the dark corner. It was very dark in there

still. There was a pile of straw on the floor and straw heaped
in the corner. And some huge thing moved ponderously. I
nearly yelped. Then I saw what it was. It was a cow.
Honestly. A sleepy fawn cow with a soft mild face like
somebody's dream woman.

"She never frew no bomb," Chalky said. He was my rifleman. Cool as ice. His voice must have broken the fellow's
nerve. There was a huge rustle in the straw in the corner
behind the cow and a man stood up, a man in a white dhoti,
young, thin, sort of smiling. Discoloured teeth. Chalky
lunged his bayonet. The chap still had plenty of nerve left.
He just swayed a little.

"Please," he said. "Have you got a smoke upon you?"

"Watch him, White," I said. I searched him.

"Please," he said. "I have nothing." He was breathing
quickly and smiling.

"Come on," I said. "Quietly."

"You know you are taking me to my death?" he said. "No
doubt?"

"I'm taking you to Poona," I said. "You killed three of our
men."

The smile sort of congealed on his face. Like a trick. His
head nodded like an old doll. "Did I?" he said. "Three men
died? Did I?"

"Come on," I said. "It's daylight."

"It's dreadful," he said. He looked sick. I felt sorry for him,
nodding his head and sick, sallow. Looked like a student,
I should say.

"Keep your hands up," Chalky said, prodding him in the
back.

We went quietly down the street, no incident at all, and
I signalled the two enveloping sections together and we got
down the road out of sight. I was in a cold sweat and I
wanted to laugh.

The trucks weren't there. God, I cursed them, waiting there. They might bitch the whole show. The villagers were going to the well quite close.

"What did you do it for, mate?" I heard Bottomley ask.

After a long silence the chap said very quietly, "For my country."

Chalky said, "Everybody says that. Beats me." Then we heard the trucks, and Chalky said, "We ought to be there in time for breakfast, boys."

THE SHADOW IN THE ROSE GARDEN

By D. H. Lawrence

A rather small young man sat by the window of a pretty seaside cottage trying to persuade himself that he was reading the newspaper. It was about half-past eight in the morning. Outside, the glory roses hung in the morning sunshine like little bowls of fire tipped up. The young man looked at the table, then at the clock, then at his own big silver watch. An expression of stiff endurance came on to his face. Then he rose and reflected on the oil-paintings that hung on the walls of the room, giving careful but hostile attention to "The Stag at Bay." He tried the lid of the piano, and found it locked. He caught sight of his own face in a little mirror, pulled his brown moustache, and an alert interest sprang into his eyes. He was not ill-favoured. He twisted his moustache. His figure was rather small, but alert and vigorous. As he turned from the mirror a look of self-commiseration mingled with his appreciation of his own physiognomy.

In a state of self-suppression, he went through into the garden. His jacket, however, did not look dejected. It was new, and had a smart and self-confident air, sitting upon a confident body. He contemplated the Tree of Heaven that flourished by the lawn, then sauntered on to the next plant. There was more promise in a crooked apple tree covered

177

with brown-red fruit. Glancing round, he broke off an apple and, with his back to the house, took a clean, sharp bite. To his surprise the fruit was sweet. He took another. Then again he turned to survey the bedroom windows overlooking the garden. He started, seeing a woman's figure; but it was only his wife. She was gazing across to the sea, apparently ignorant of him.

For a moment or two he looked at her, watching her. She was a good-looking woman, who seemed older than he, rather pale, but healthy, her face yearning. Her rich auburn hair was heaped in folds on her forehead. She looked apart from him and his world, gazing away to the sea. It irked her husband that she should continue abstracted and in ignorance of him; he pulled poppy fruits and threw them at the window. She started, glanced at him with a wild smile, and looked away again. Then almost immediately she left the window. He went indoors to meet her. She had a fine carriage, very proud, and wore a dress of soft white muslin.

"I've been waiting long enough," he said.

"For me or for breakfast?" she said lightly. "You know we said nine o'clock. I should have thought you could have slept after the journey."

"You know I'm always up at five, and I couldn't stop in bed after six. You might as well be in pit as in bed, on a morning like this."

"I shouldn't have thought the pit would occur to you, here."

She moved about examining the room, looking at the ornaments under glass covers. He, planted on the hearthrug, watched her rather uneasily, and grudgingly indulgent. She shrugged her shoulders at the apartment.

"Come," she said, taking his arm, "let us go into the garden till Mrs. Coates brings the tray."

"I hope she'll be quick," he said, pulling his moustache.

She gave a short laugh, and leaned on his arm as they went. He had lighted a pipe.

Mrs. Coates entered the room as they went down the steps. The delightful, erect old lady hastened to the window for a good view of her visitors. Her china-blue eyes were bright as she watched the young couple go down the path, he walking in an easy, confident fashion, with his wife on his arm. The landlady began talking to herself in a soft, Yorkshire accent.

"Just of a height they are. She wouldn't ha' married a man less than herself in stature, I think, though he's not her equal otherwise." Here her granddaughter came in, setting a tray on the table. The girl went to the old woman's side.

"He's been eating the apples, gran'," she said.

"Has he, my pet? Well, if he's happy, why not?"

Outside, the young well-favoured man listened with impatience to the chink of the teacups. At last, with a sigh of relief, the couple came in to breakfast. After he had eaten for some time, he rested a moment and said:

"Do you think it's any better place than Bridlington?"

"I do," she said, "infinitely! Besides, I am at home here — it's not like a strange sea-side place to me."

"How long were you here?"

"Two years."

He ate reflectively.

"I should ha' thought you'd rather go to a fresh place," he said at length.

She sat very silent, and then, delicately, put out a feeler.

"Why?" she said. "Do you think I shan't enjoy myself?"

He laughed comfortably, putting the marmalade thick on his bread.

"I hope so," he said.

She again took no notice of him.

"But don't say anything about it in the village, Frank,"

she said casually. "Don't say who I am, or that I used to live here. There's nobody I want to meet, particularly, and we should never feel free if they knew me again."

"Why did you come, then?"

" 'Why?' Can't you understand why?"

"Not if you don't want to know anybody."

"I came to see the place, not the people."

He did not say any more.

"Women," she said, "are different from men. I don't know why I wanted to come — but I did."

She helped him to another cup of coffee, solicitously.

"Only," she resumed, "don't talk about me in the village." She laughed shakily. "I don't want my past brought up against me, you know." And she moved the crumbs on the cloth with her finger-tip.

He looked at her as he drank his coffee; he sucked his moustache, and putting down his cup, said phlegmatically:

"I'll bet you've had a lot of past."

She looked with a little guiltiness, that flattered him, down at the tablecloth.

"Well," she said, caressive, "you won't give me away, who I am, will you?"

"No," he said, comforting, laughing, "I won't give you away."

He was pleased.

She remained silent. After a moment or two she lifted her head, saying:

"I've got to arrange with Mrs. Coates, and do various things. So you'd better go out by yourself this morning — and we'll be in to dinner at one."

"But you can't be arranging with Mrs. Coates all morning," he said.

"Oh, well — then I've some letters to write, and I must get

that mark out of my skirt. I've got plenty of little things to do this morning. You'd better go out by yourself."

He perceived that she wanted to be rid of him, so that when she went upstairs, he took his hat and lounged out on to the cliffs, suppressedly angry.

Presently she too came out. She wore a hat with roses, and a long lace scarf hung over her white dress. Rather nervously, she put up her sunshade, and her face was half-hidden in its coloured shadow. She went along the narrow track of flag-stones that were worn hollow by the feet of the fishermen. She seemed to be avoiding her surroundings, as if she remained safe in the little obscurity of her parasol.

She passed the church, and went down the lane till she came to a high wall by the wayside. Under this she went slowly, stopping at length by an open doorway, which shone like a picture of light in the dark wall. There in the magic beyond the doorway, patterns of shadow lay on the sunny court, on the blue and white sea-pebbles of its paving, while a green lawn glowed beyond, where a bay tree glittered at the edges. She tiptoed nervously into the courtyard, glancing at the house that stood in shadow. The uncurtained windows looked black and soulless, the kitchen door stood open. Irresolutely she took a step forward, and again forward, leaning, yearning, towards the garden beyond.

She had almost gained the corner of the house when a heavy step came crunching through the trees. A gardener appeared before her. He held a wicker tray on which were rolling great, dark red gooseberries, overripe. He moved slowly.

"The garden isn't open to-day," he said quietly to the attractive woman, who was poised for retreat.

For a moment she was silent with surprise. How should it be public at all?

"When is it open?" she asked, quick-witted.

"The rector lets visitors in on Fridays and Tuesdays."

She stood still, reflecting. How strange to think of the rector opening his garden to the public!

"But everybody will be at church," she said coaxingly to the man. "There'll be nobody here, will there?"

He moved, and the big gooseberries rolled.

"The rector lives at the new rectory," he said.

The two stood still. He did not like to ask her to go. At last she turned to him with a winning smile.

"Might I have *one* peep at the roses?" she coaxed, with pretty wilfulness.

"I don't suppose it would matter," he said, moving aside; "you won't stop long —"

She went forward, forgetting the gardener in a moment. Her face became strained, her movements eager. Glancing round, she saw all the windows giving on to the lawn were curtainless and dark. The house had a sterile appearance, as if it were still used, but not inhabited. A shadow seemed to go over her. She went across the lawn towards the garden, through an arch of crimson ramblers, a gate of colour. There beyond lay the soft blue sea within the bay, misty with morning, and the furthest headland of black rock jutting dimly out between blue and blue of the sky and water. Her face began to shine, transfigured with pain and joy. At her feet the garden fell steeply, all a confusion of flowers, and away below was the darkness of tree-tops covering the beck.

She turned to the garden that shone with sunny flowers around her. She knew the little corner where was the seat beneath the yew tree. Then there was the terrace where a great host of flowers shone, and from this, two paths went down, one at each side of the garden. She closed her sunshade and walked slowly among the many flowers. All round were rose bushes, big banks of roses, then roses hanging

and tumbling from pillars, or roses balanced on the standard
bushes. By the open earth were many other flowers. If
she lifted her head, the sea was upraised beyond, and
the Cape.

Slowly she went down one path, lingering, like one who
has gone back into the past. Suddenly she was touching
some heavy crimson roses that were soft as velvet, touching
them thoughtfully, without knowing, as a mother sometimes
fondles the hand of her child. She leaned slightly forward
to catch the scent. Then she wandered on in abstraction.
Sometimes a flame-coloured, scentless rose would hold her
arrested. She stood gazing at it as if she could not understand it. Again the same softness of intimacy came over her,
as she stood before a tumbling heap of pink petals. Then
she wondered over the white rose, that was greenish, like
ice, in the centre. So, slowly, like a white, pathetic butterfly,
she drifted down the path, coming at last to a tiny terrace
all full of roses. They seemed to fill the place, a sunny, gay
throng. She was shy of them, they were so many and so
bright. They seemed to be conversing and laughing. She
felt herself in a strange crowd. It exhilarated her, carried her
out of herself. She flushed with excitement. The air was pure
scent.

Hastily, she went to a little seat among the white roses,
and sat down. Her scarlet sunshade made a hard blot of
colour. She sat quite still, feeling her own existence lapse.
She was no more than a rose, a rose that could not quite
come into blossom, but remained tense. A little fly dropped
on her knee, on her white dress. She watched it, as if it had
fallen on a rose. She was not herself.

Then she started cruelly as a shadow crossed her and a
figure moved into her sight. It was a man who had come in
slippers, unheard. He wore a linen coat. The morning was
shattered, the spell vanished away. She was only afraid of

being questioned. He came forward. She rose. Then, seeing
him, the strength went from her and she sank on the seat
again.

He was a young man, military in appearance, growing
slightly stout. His black hair was brushed smooth and bright,
his moustache was waxed. But there was something ram-
bling in his gait. She looked up, blanched to the lips, and
saw his eyes. They were black, and stared without seeing.
They were not a man's eyes. He was coming towards her.

He stared at her fixedly, made an unconscious salute,
and sat down beside her on the seat. He moved on the
bench, shifted his feet, saying, in a gentlemanly, military
voice:

"I don't disturb you — do I?"

She was mute and helpless. He was scrupulously dressed
in dark clothes and a linen coat. She could not move. Seeing
his hands, with the ring she knew so well upon the little
finger, she felt as if she were going dazed. The whole world
was deranged. She sat unavailing. For his hands, her sym-
bols of passionate love, filled her with horror as they rested
now on his strong thighs.

"May I smoke?" he asked intimately, almost secretly, his
hand going to his pocket.

She could not answer, but it did not matter, he was in
another world. She wondered, craving, if he recognized her
— if he could recognize her. She sat pale with anguish.
But she had to go through it.

"I haven't got any tobacco," he said thoughtfully.

But she paid no heed to his words, only she attended to
him. Could he recognize her, or was it all gone? She sat still
in a frozen kind of suspense.

"I smoke John Cotton," he said, "and I must economize
with it, it is expensive. You know, I'm not very well off while
these lawsuits are going on."

"No," she said, and her heart was cold, her soul kept rigid.

He moved, made a loose salute, rose, and went away. She sat motionless. She could see his shape, the shape she had loved with all her passion: his compact, soldier's head, his fine figure now slackened. And it was not he. It only filled her with horror too difficult to know.

Suddenly he came again, his hand in his jacket pocket.

"Do you mind if I smoke?" he said. "Perhaps I shall be able to see things more clearly."

He sat down beside her again, filling a pipe. She watched his hands with the fine strong fingers. They had always inclined to tremble slightly. It had surprised her, long ago, in such a healthy man. Now they moved inaccurately, and the tobacco hung raggedly out of the pipe.

"I have legal business to attend to. Legal affairs are always so uncertain. I tell my solicitor exactly, precisely what I want, but I can never get it done."

She sat and heard him talking. But it was not he. Yet those were the hands she had kissed, there were the glistening, strange black eyes that she had loved. Yet it was not he. She sat motionless with horror and silence. He dropped his tobacco pouch, and groped for it on the ground. Yet she must wait to see if he would recognize her. Why could she not go! In a moment he rose.

"I must go at once," he said. "The owl is coming." Then he added confidentially: "His name isn't really the owl, but I call him that. I must go and see if he has come."

She rose too. He stood before her, uncertain. He was a handsome, soldierly fellow, and a lunatic. Her eyes searched him, and searched him, to see if he would recognize her, if she could discover him.

"You don't know me?" she asked, from the terror of her soul, standing alone.

He looked back at her quizzically. She had to bear his eyes. They gleamed on her, but with no intelligence. He was drawing nearer to her.

"Yes, I do know you," he said, fixed, intent, but mad, drawing his face nearer hers. Her horror was too great. The powerful lunatic was coming too near to her.

A man approached, hastening.

"The garden isn't open this morning," he said.

The deranged man stopped and looked at him. The keeper went to the seat and picked up the tobacco pouch left lying there.

"Don't leave your tobacco, sir," he said, taking it to the gentleman in the linen coat.

"I was just asking this lady to stay to lunch," the latter said politely. "She is a friend of mine."

The woman turned and walked swiftly, blindly, between the sunny roses, out from the garden, past the house with the blank, dark windows, through the sea-pebbled court-yard to the street. Hastening and blind, she went forward without hesitating, not knowing whither. Directly she came to the house she went upstairs, took off her hat, and sat down on the bed. It was as if some membrane had been torn in two in her, so that she was not an entity that could think and feel. She sat staring across at the window, where an ivy spray waved slowly up and down in the sea wind. There was some of the uncanny luminousness of the sunlit sea in the air. She sat perfectly still, without any being. She only felt she might be sick, and it might be blood that was loose in her torn entrails. She sat perfectly still and passive.

After a time she heard the hard tread of her husband on the floor below, and, without herself changing, she registered his movement. She heard his rather disconsolate footsteps go out again, then his voice speaking, answering, growing cheery, and his solid tread drawing near.

He entered, ruddy, rather pleased, an air of complacency about his alert, sturdy figure. She moved stiffly. He faltered in his approach.

"What's the matter?" he asked, a tinge of impatience in his voice. "Aren't you feeling well?"

This was torture to her.

"Quite," she replied.

His brown eyes became puzzled and angry.

"What is the matter?" he said.

"Nothing."

He took a few strides, and stood obstinately, looking out of the window.

"Have you run up against anybody?" he asked.

"Nobody who knows me," she said.

His hands began to twitch. It exasperated him, that she was no more sensible of him than if he did not exist. Turning on her at length, driven, he asked:

"Something has upset you, hasn't it?"

"No, why?" she said, neutral. He did not exist for her, except as an irritant.

His anger rose, filling the veins in his throat.

"It seems like it," he said, making an effort not to show his anger, because there seemed no reason for it. He went away downstairs. She sat still on the bed, and with the residue of feeling left to her, she disliked him because he tormented her. The time went by. She could smell the dinner being served, the smoke of her husband's pipe from the garden. But she could not move. She had no being. There was a tinkle of the bell. She heard him come indoors. And then he mounted the stairs again. At every step her heart grew tight in her. He opened the door.

"Dinner is on the table," he said.

It was difficult for her to endure his presence, for he would interfere with her. She could not recover her life.

She rose stiffly and went down. She could neither eat nor talk during the meal. She sat absent, torn, without any being of her own. He tried to go on as if nothing were the matter. But at last he became silent with fury. As soon as it was possible, she went upstairs again, and locked the bedroom door. She must be alone. He went with his pipe into the garden. All his suppressed anger against her who held herself superior to him filled and blackened his heart. Though he had not known it, yet he had never really won her, she had never loved him. She had taken him on sufferance. This had foiled him. He was only a labouring electrician in the mine, she was superior to him. He had always given way to her. But all the while, the injury and ignominy had been working in his soul because she did not hold him seriously. And now all his rage came up against her.

He turned and went indoors. The third time, she heard him mounting the stairs. Her heart stood still. He turned the catch and pushed the door — it was locked. He tried it again, harder. Her heart was standing still.

"Have you fastened the door?" he asked quietly, because of the landlady.

"Yes. Wait a minute."

She rose and turned the lock, afraid he would burst it. She felt hatred towards him, because he did not leave her free. He entered, his pipe between his teeth, and she returned to her old position on the bed. He closed the door and stood with his back to it.

"What's the matter?" he asked determinedly.

She was sick with him. She could not look at him.

"Can't you leave me alone?" she replied, averting her face from him.

He looked at her quickly, fully, wincing with ignominy. Then he seemed to consider for a moment.

"There's something up with you, isn't there?" he asked definitely.

"Yes," she said, "but that's no reason why you should torment me."

"I don't torment you. What's the matter?"

"Why should you know?" she cried, in hate and desperation.

Something snapped. He started and caught his pipe as it fell from his mouth. Then he pushed forward the bitten-off mouthpiece with his tongue, took it from off his lips, and looked at it. Then he put out his pipe, and brushed the ash from his waistcoat. After which he raised his head.

"I want to know," he said. His face was greyish pale, and set uglily.

Neither looked at the other. She knew he was fired now. His heart was pounding heavily. She hated him, but she could not withstand him. Suddenly she lifted her head and turned on him.

"What right have you to know?" she asked.

He looked at her. She felt a pang of surprise for his tortured eyes and his fixed face. But her heart hardened swiftly. She had never loved him. She did not love him now.

But suddenly she lifted her head again swiftly, like a thing that tries to get free. She wanted to be free of it. It was not him so much, but it, something she had put on herself, that bound her so horribly. And having put the bond on herself, it was hardest to take it off. But now she hated everything and felt destructive. He stood with his back to the door, fixed, as if he would oppose her eternally, till she was extinguished. She looked at him. Her eyes were cold and hostile. His workman's hands spread on the panels of the door behind him.

"You know I used to live here?" she began, in a hard voice,

as if wilfully to wound him. He braced himself against her,
and nodded.

"Well, I was companion to Miss Birch of Torril Hall —
she and the rector were friends, and Archie was the rector's
son." There was a pause. He listened without knowing what
was happening. He stared at his wife. She was squatted in
her white dress on the bed, carefully folding and re-folding
the hem of her skirt. Her voice was full of hostility.

"He was an officer — a sub-lieutenant — then he quar-
relled with his colonel and came out of the army. At any
rate"— she plucked at her skirt hem, her husband stood
motionless, watching her movements which filled his veins
with madness —"he was awfully fond of me, and I was of
him — awfully."

"How old was he?" asked the husband.

"When — when I first knew him? Or when he went
away? —"

"When you first knew him."

"When I first knew him, he was twenty-six — now — he's
thirty-one — nearly thirty-two — because I'm twenty-nine,
and he is nearly three years older —"

She lifted her head and looked at the opposite wall.

"And what then?" said her husband.

She hardened herself, and said callously:

"We were as good as engaged for nearly a year, though
nobody knew — at least — they talked — but — it wasn't
open. Then he went away — "

"He chucked you?" said the husband brutally, wanting to
hurt her into contact with himself. Her heart rose wildly
with rage. Then "Yes," she said, to anger him. He shifted
from one foot to the other, giving a "Ph!" of rage. There was
silence for a time.

"Then," she resumed, her pain giving a mocking note to
her words, "he suddenly went out to fight in Africa, and

almost the very day I first met you, I heard from Miss Birch he'd got sunstroke — and two months after, that he was dead — "

"That was before you took on with me?" said the husband.

There was no answer. Neither spoke for a time. He had not understood. His eyes were contracted uglily.

"So you've been looking at your old courting places!" he said. "That was what you wanted to go out by yourself for this morning."

Still she did not answer him anything. He went away from the door to the window. He stood with his hands behind him, his back to her. She looked at him. His hands seemed gross to her, the back of his head paltry.

At length, almost against his will, he turned round, asking:

"How long were you carrying on with him?"

"What do you mean?" she replied coldly.

"I mean how long were you carrying on with him?"

She lifted her head, averting her face from him. She refused to answer. Then she said:

"I don't know what you mean, by carrying on. I loved him from the first days I met him — two months after I went to stay with Miss Birch."

"And do you reckon he loved you?" he jeered.

"I know he did."

"How do you know, if he'd have no more to do with you?"

There was a long silence of hate and suffering.

"And how far did it go between you?" he asked at length, in a frightened, stiff voice.

"I hate your not-straightforward questions," she cried, beside herself with his baiting. "We loved each other, and we *were* lovers — we were. I don't care what *you* think: what have you got to do with it? We were lovers before ever I knew you — "

"Lovers — lovers," he said, white with fury. "You mean

you had your fling with an army man, and then came to me
to marry you when you'd done — "

She sat swallowing her bitterness. There was a long pause.

"Do you mean to say you used to go — the whole hogger?"
he asked, still incredulous.

"Why, what else do you think I mean?" she cried brutally.

He shrank, and became white, impersonal. There was a
long, paralysed silence. He seemed to have gone small.

"You never thought to tell me all this before I married
you," he said, with bitter irony, at last.

"You never asked me," she replied.

"I never thought there was any need."

"Well, then, you *should* think."

He stood with expressionless, almost childlike set face,
revolving many thoughts, whilst his heart was mad with
anguish.

Suddenly she added:

"And I saw him to-day," she said. "He is not dead, he's
mad."

Her husband looked at her, startled.

"Mad!" he said involuntarily.

"A lunatic," she said. It almost cost her her reason to utter
the word. There was a pause.

"Did he know you?" asked the husband, in a small voice.

"No," she said.

He stood and looked at her. At last he had learned the
width of the breach between them. She still squatted on the
bed. He could not go near her. It would be violation to each
of them to be brought into contact with the other. The thing
must work itself out. They were both shocked so much, they
were impersonal, and no longer hated each other. After some
minutes he left her and went out.

A WORN PATH

By Eudora Welty

It was December — a bright frozen day in the early morning. Far out in the country there was an old Negro woman with her head tied in a red rag, coming along a path through the pinewoods. Her name was Phoenix Jackson. She was very old and small and she walked slowly in the dark pine shadows, moving a little from side to side in her steps, with the balanced heaviness and lightness of a pendulum in a grandfather clock. She carried a thin, small cane made from an umbrella, and with this she kept tapping the frozen earth in front of her. This made a grave and persistent noise in the still air, that seemed meditative, like the chirping of a solitary little bird.

She wore a dark striped dress reaching down to her shoe-tops, and an equally long apron of bleached sugar sacks, with a full pocket; all neat and tidy, but every time she took a step she might have fallen over her shoe-laces, which dragged from her unlaced shoes. She looked straight ahead. Her eyes were blue with age. Her skin had a pattern all its own of numberless branching wrinkles and as though a whole little tree stood in the middle of her forehead, but a golden colour ran underneath, and the two knobs of her cheeks were illuminated by a yellow burning under the dark. Under the red rag her hair came down on her neck in the frailest of ringlets, still black, and with an odour like copper.

Now and then there was a quivering in the thicket. Old Phoenix said, "Out of my way, all you foxes, owls, beetles, jack rabbits, coons and wild animals! . . . Keep out from under these feet, little bob-whites. . . . Keep the big wild hogs out of my path. Don't let none of those come running my direction. I got a long way." Under her small black-freckled hand her cane, limber as a buggy whip, would switch at the brush as if to rouse up any hiding things.

On she went. The woods were deep and still. The sun made the pine needles almost too bright to look at, up where the wind rocked. The cones dropped as light as feathers. Down in the hollow was the mourning dove — it was not too late for him.

The path ran up a hill. "Seem like there is chains about my feet, time I get this far," she said, in the voice of argument old people keep to use with themselves. "Something always take a hold of me on this hill — pleads I should stay."

After she got to the top she turned and gave a full, severe look behind her where she had come. "Up through pines," she said at length. "Now down through oaks."

Her eyes opened their widest, and she started down gently. But before she got to the bottom of the hill a bush caught her dress.

Her fingers were busy and intent, but her skirts were full and long, so that before she could pull them free in one place they were caught in another. It was not possible to allow the dress to tear. "I in the thorny bush," she said. "Thorns, you doing your appointed work. Never want to let folks pass, no sir. Old eyes thought you was a pretty little *green* bush."

Finally, trembling all over, she stood free, and after a moment dared to stoop for her cane.

"Sun so high!" she cried, leaning back and looking, while the thick tears went over her eyes. "The time getting all gone here."

At the foot of this hill was a place where a log was laid across the creek.

"Now comes the trial," said Phoenix.

Putting her right foot out, she mounted the log and shut her eyes. Lifting her skirt, levelling her cane fiercely before her, like a festival figure in some parade, she began to march across. Then she opened her eyes and she was safe on the other side.

"I wasn't as old as I thought," she said.

But she sat down to rest. She spread her skirts on the bank around her and folded her hands over her knees. Up above her was a tree in a pearly cloud of mistletoe. She did not dare to close her eyes, and when a little boy brought her a little plate with a slice of marble-cake on it she spoke to him. "That would be acceptable," she said. But when she went to take it there was just her own hand in the air.

So she left that tree, and had to go through a barbed-wire fence. There she had to creep and crawl, spreading her knees and stretching her fingers like a baby trying to climb the steps. But she talked loudly to herself: she could not let her dress be torn now, so late in the day, and she could not pay for having her arm or her leg sawed off if she got caught fast where she was.

At last she was safe through the fence and risen up out in the clearing. Big dead trees, like black men with one arm, were standing in the purple stalks of the withered cotton field. There sat a buzzard.

"Who you watching?"

In the furrow she made her way along.

"Glad this not the season for bulls," she said, looking sideways, "and the good Lord made his snakes to curl up and sleep in the winter. A pleasure I don't see no two-headed snake coming round that tree, where it come once. It took a while to get by him, back in the summer."

She passed through the old cotton and went into a field of dead corn. It whispered and shook and was taller than her head. "Through the maze now," she said, for there was no path.

Then there was something tall, black, and skinny there, moving before her.

At first she took it for a man. It could have been a man dancing in the field. But she stood still and listened, and it did not make a sound. It was as silent as a ghost.

"Ghost," she said sharply, "who be you the ghost of? For I have heard of nary death close by."

But there was no answer — only the ragged dancing in the wind.

She shut her eyes, reached out her hand, and touched a sleeve. She found a coat and inside that an emptiness, cold as ice.

"You scarecrow," she said. Her face lighted. "I ought to be shut up for good," she said with laughter. "My senses is gone. I too old. I the oldest people I ever know. Dance, old scarecrow," she said, "while I dancing with you."

She kicked her foot over the furrow, and with mouth drawn down, shook her head once or twice in a little strutting way. Some husks blew down and whirled in streamers about her skirts.

Then she went on, parting her way from side to side with the cane, through the whispering field. At last she came to the end, to a wagon track where the silver grass blew between the red ruts. The quail were walking around like pullets, seeming all dainty and unseen.

"Walk pretty," she said. "This the easy place. This the easy going."

She followed the track, swaying through the quiet bare fields, through the little strings of trees silver in their dead leaves, past cabins silver from weather, with the doors and windows boarded shut, all like old women under a spell sitting there. "I walking in their sleep," she said, nodding her head vigorously.

In a ravine she went where a spring was silently flowing through a hollow log. Old Phoenix bent and drank. "Sweet-gum makes the water sweet," she said, and drank more. "Nobody knows who made this well, for it was here when I was born."

The track crossed a swampy part where the moss hung as white as lace from every limb. "Sleep on, alligators, and blow your bubbles." Then the track went into the road.

Deep, deep the road went down between the high green-coloured banks. Overhead the live-oaks met, and it was as dark as a cave.

A black dog with a lolling tongue came up out of the weeds by the ditch. She was meditating, and not ready, and when he came at her she only hit him a little with her cane. Over she went in the ditch, like a little puff of milk-weed.

Down there, her senses drifted away. A dream visited her, and she reached her hand up, but nothing reached down and gave her a pull. So she lay there and presently went to talking. "Old woman," she said to herself, "that black dog come up out of the weeds to stall you off, and now there he sitting on his fine tail, smiling at you."

A white man finally came along and found her — a hunter, a young man, with his dog on a chain.

"Well, Granny!" he laughed. "What are you doing there?"

"Lying on my back like a June-bug waiting to be turned over, mister," she said, reaching up her hand.

He lifted her up, gave her a swing in the air, and set her down. "Anything broken, Granny?"

"No, sir, them old dead weeds is springy enough," said
Phoenix, when she had got her breath. "I thank you for your
trouble."

"Where do you live, Granny?" he asked, while the two
dogs were growling at each other.

"Away back yonder, sir, behind the ridge. You can't even
see it from here."

"On your way home?"

"No, sir, I going to town."

"Why, that's too far! That's as far as I walk when I come
out myself, and I get something for my trouble." He patted
the stuffed bag he carried, and there hung down a little
closed claw. It was one of the bob-whites, with its beak
hooked bitterly to show it was dead. "Now you go on home,
Granny!"

"I bound to go to town, mister," said Phoenix. "The time
come round."

He gave another laugh, filling the whole landscape. "I
know you old coloured people! Wouldn't miss going to town
to see Santa Claus!"

But something held old Phoenix very still. The deep lines
in her face went into a fierce and different radiation. Without warning, she had seen with her own eyes a flashing
nickel fall out of the man's pocket on to the ground.

"How old are you, Granny?" he was saying.

"There is no telling, mister," she said, "no telling."

Then she gave a little cry and clapped her hands and said,
"Git on away from here, dog! Look! Look at that dog!" She
laughed as if in admiration. "He ain't scared of nobody. He
a big black dog." She whispered, "Sic him!"

"Watch me get rid of that cur," said the man. "Sic him,
Pete! Sic him!"

Phoenix heard the dogs fighting, and heard the man running and throwing sticks. She even heard a gunshot. But

she was slowly bending forward by that time, further and further forward, the lids stretched down over her eyes, as if she were doing this in her sleep. Her chin was lowered almost to her knees. The yellow palm of her hand came out from the fold of her apron. Her fingers slid down and along the ground under the piece of money with the grace and care they would have in lifting an egg from under a sitting hen. Then she slowly straightened up, she stood erect, and the nickel was in her apron pocket. A bird flew by. Her lips moved. "God watching me the whole time. I come to stealing."

The man came back, and his own dog panted about them. "Well, I scared him off that time," he said, and then he laughed and lifted his gun and pointed it at Phoenix.

She stood straight and faced him.

"Doesn't the gun scare you?" he said, still pointing it.

"No, sir, I seen plenty go off closer by, in my day, and for less than what I done," she said, holding utterly still.

He smiled, and shouldered the gun. "Well, Granny," he said, "you must be a hundred years old, and scared of noth-ing. I'd give you a dime if I had any money with me. But you take my advice and stay home, and nothing will happen to you."

"I bound to go on my way, mister," said Phoenix. She inclined her head in the red rag. Then they went in different directions, but she could hear the gun shooting again and again over the hill.

She walked on. The shadows hung from the oak trees to the road like curtains. Then she smelled wood-smoke, and smelled the river, and she saw a steeple and the cabins on their steep steps. Dozens of little black children whirled around her. There ahead was Natchez shining. Bells were ringing. She walked on.

In the paved city it was Christmas time. There were red

and green electric lights strung and criss-crossed everywhere, and all turned on in the daytime. Old Phoenix would
have been lost if she had not distrusted her eyesight and
depended on her feet to know where to take her.

She paused quietly on the sidewalk where people were
passing by. A lady came along in the crowd, carrying an
armful of red-, green-, and silver-wrapped presents; she
gave off perfume like the red roses in hot summer, and
Phoenix stopped her.

"Please, missy, will you lace up my shoe?" she held up
her foot.

"What do you want, Grandma?"

"See my shoe," said Phoenix. "Do all right for out in the
country, but wouldn't look right to go in a big building."

"Stand still then, Grandma," said the lady. She put her
packages down on the sidewalk beside her and laced and
tied both shoes tightly.

"Can't lace 'em with a cane," said Phoenix. "Thank you,
missy. I doesn't mind asking a nice lady to tie up my shoe,
when I gets out on the street."

Moving slowly and from side to side, she went into the
big building, and into a tower of steps, where she walked
up and round and round until her feet knew to stop.

She entered a door, and there she saw nailed up on the
wall the document that had been stamped with the gold seal
and framed in the gold frame, which matched the dream
that was hung up in her head.

"Here I be," she said. There was a fixed and ceremonial
stiffness over her body.

"A charity case, I suppose," said an attendant who sat at
the desk before her.

But Phoenix only looked above her head. There was sweat
on her face, the wrinkles in her skin shone like a bright net.

"Speak up, Grandma," the woman said. "What's your

name? We must have your history, you know. Have you been here before? What seems to be the trouble with you?"

Old Phoenix only gave a twitch to her face as if a fly were bothering her.

"Are you deaf?" cried the attendant.

But then the nurse came in.

"Oh, that's just old Aunt Phoenix," she said. "She doesn't come for herself — she has a little grandson. She makes these trips just as regular as clockwork. She lives away back off the Old Natchez Trace." She bent down. "Well, Aunt Phoenix, why don't you just take a seat? We won't keep you standing after your long trip." She pointed.

The old woman sat down, bolt upright in the chair.

"Now, how is the boy?" asked the nurse.

Old Phoenix did not speak.

"I said, how is the boy?"

But Phoenix only waited and stared straight ahead, her face very solemn and withdrawn into rigidity.

"Is his throat any better?" asked the nurse. "Aunt Phoenix, don't you hear me? Is your grandson's throat any better since the last time you came for the medicine?"

With her hands on her knees, the old woman waited, silent, erect and motionless, just as if she were in armour.

"You mustn't take up our time this way, Aunt Phoenix," the nurse said. "Tell us quickly about your grandson, and get it over. He isn't dead, is he?"

At last there came a flicker and then a flame of comprehension across her face, and she spoke.

"My grandson. It was my memory had left me. There I sat and forgot why I made my long trip."

"Forgot?" The nurse frowned. "After you came so far?"

Then Phoenix was like an old woman begging a dignified forgiveness for waking up frightened in the night. "I never did go to school, I was too old at the Surrender," she said in a soft voice. "I'm an old woman without an education. It was my memory fail me. My little grandson he is just the same, and I forgot it in the coming."

"Throat never heals, does it?" said the nurse, speaking in a loud, sure voice to old Phoenix. By now she had a card with something written on it, a little list. "Yes. Swallowed lye. When was it? — January — two-three years ago — "

Phoenix spoke unasked now. "No, missy, he not dead, he just the same. Every little while his throat begin to close up again, and he not able to swallow. He not get his breath. He not able to help himself. So the time come round, and I go on another trip for the soothing medicine."

"All right. The doctor said as long as you came to get it, you could have it," said the nurse. "But it's an obstinate case."

"My little grandson, he sits up there in the house all wrapped up, waiting by himself," Phoenix went on. "We is the only two left in the world. He suffer and it don't seem to put him back at all. He got a sweet look. He going to last. He wear a little patch quilt and peep out holding his mouth open like a little bird. I remembers so plain now. I not going to forget him again, no, the whole enduring time. I could tell him from all the others in creation."

"All right." The nurse was trying to hush her now. She brought her a bottle of medicine. "Charity," she said, making a check mark in the book.

Old Phoenix held the bottle close to her eyes, and then carefully put it into her pocket.

"I thank you," she said.

"It's Christmas time, Grandma," said the attendant. "Could I give you a few pennies out of my purse?"

"Five pennies is a nickel," said Phoenix stiffly.

"Here's a nickel," said the attendant.

Phoenix rose carefully and held out her hand. She

received the nickel and then fished the other nickel out of her pocket and laid it beside the new one. She stared at her palm closely, with her head on one side.

Then she gave a tap with her cane on the floor.

"This is what come to me to do," she said. "I going to the store and buy my child a little windmill they sells, made out of paper. He going to find it hard to believe there such a thing in the world. I'll march myself back where he waiting, holding it straight up in this hand."

She lifted her free hand, gave a little nod, turned round, and walked out of the doctor's office. Then her slow step began on the stairs, going down.

NOTES ON THE AUTHORS

KAY BOYLE (1903–   ). Born in St. Paul, Minnesota, Kay Boyle has lived much in Europe and has made of her fiction — both short stories and novels — an instrument for recording with brilliance and power the many kinds of life she has witnessed there — the lives both of Europeans and of Americans abroad —in the years between the wars and during the first years of the last war. Hers has always been a name to conjure with in the little magazines and in the more determinedly literary reviews, but she is also well known to readers of *The Saturday Evening Post* and *The New Yorker*. Her latest novel is *His Human Majesty* (1949). *The Crazy Hunter* (1940) consists of three brilliant short novels.

ANTON CHEKHOV (1860–1904). Chekhov, a native of the Ukraine, took a medical degree at the University of Moscow in 1884, but he early discovered that he had a stronger vocation for letters than for medicine, and never took up formal practice. His first stories were humorous sketches, which had a considerable degree of success, but before long he was writing his more characteristically serious stories. His plays, of which the best known are *The Sea Gull* (1896), *Uncle Vanya* (1899), *The Three Sisters* (1901), and *The Cherry Orchard* (1904), no doubt form the mainstay of his reputation, but his many short stories, in which he achieves the highest degree of subtle expressiveness and human understanding, have been an influence of the first importance in the subsequent development of the short story, not only on the Continent but also in England and America. Chekhov developed consumption early in life, and made frequent sojourns in the Crimea in an effort to regain his health. In 1903, he made the same desperate journey to Badenweiler, in Germany's Black Forest, that Stephen Crane had made in 1900; like Crane, he died there.

STEPHEN CRANE (1871–1900). Crane's short life was full of movement, color, and contrast. He began his career as a journalist in New York City. The first landmark to be raised in the midst of his struggle for independence was the naturalistic novel, *Maggie: A Girl of the Streets,* which Crane published at his own expense and on which he took a complete loss. With *The Red Badge of Courage,* his Civil War story of fear and bravery, published periodically in 1894 and in book form in 1895, Crane became known as the author of a great novel; more important, he himself became sure of the direction in which his vocation lay. At one time or another in the course of his brief thirty years he was a newspaper correspondent, a war correspondent in Cuba during the Spanish-American War, a foot-loose wanderer and observer in Mexico and in Greece, a kind of lord of the manor at Brede Place, Sussex, and (far from least) the friend of Joseph Conrad; always, however, whether as journalist or as the author of novels and stories, he was a writer. His last years were difficult, despite his wife's devotion; like Chekhov, he made too late the journey to Badenweiler in search of health, and died there on June 5, 1900.

THOMAS HARDY (1840–1928). Hardy began his professional life as a church architect, but soon turned to literature. The first of his many novels was published in 1871; the most widely read are probably *The Return of the Native* (1878), with its powerful, disturbing evocation of the somber Edgon Heath, and *Tess of the d'Urbervilles* (1891), with its central tragedy expressive of a bitter, thoroughgoing fatalism. His finest short stories are contained in *Wessex Tales* (1888) and *Life's Little Ironies* (1894). In his later years Hardy turned away from fiction (piqued, some say, by the public's shallow, shocked reaction to *Jude the Obscure*) and devoted himself to poetry, publishing several volumes of verse between 1898 and his death. His greatest poetic work — possibly the greatest of all his works — is *The Dynasts*, a vast dramatic panorama of the Napoleonic era, published in three parts between 1903 and 1908. The best biography is by his wife, Florence Hardy; the most interesting recent critical account is Lord David Cecil's book, *Hardy the Novelist*.

NATHANIEL HAWTHORNE (1804–1864). The facts about Hawthorne's life are too easily accessible to need recounting here. Perhaps the clearest and most detailed insight into his life and the impulses and experiences which conditioned his writing is to be obtained from *The American Notebooks of Nathaniel Hawthorne*, edited by Randall Stewart (Yale University Press, 1932). Impressions and judgments by two of his peers are afforded by Henry James's biography (1880) and by Herman Melville's essay, "One of Hawthorne's Mosses" (both conveniently accessible in Edmund Wilson's *The Shock of Recognition*).

ERNEST HEMINGWAY (1898–   ). Hemingway was born in Oak Park, Illinois. His service during the first World War with a volunteer ambulance unit in France and with the Italian infantry on the Italian front provided material for many of his short stories and for *A Farewell to Arms*. His first major novel, *The Sun Also Rises* (1926), is thought by many to be the classic description of the lives of the "lost generation" in Europe, particularly in Paris, after the first World War. *For Whom the Bell Tolls* (1940) is set against a background of the Spanish civil war; Hemingway's latest novel, *Across the River and into the Trees* (1950), against a background of the recent war in Italy. During both of those conflicts, as at other times in his career, he was a correspondent. *Death in the Afternoon* (1932) gives full play to his enthusiastic interest in bull-fighting, while *The Green Hills of Africa* (1935) describes some of his experiences as a big-game hunter. More even than with most writers who use both the novel and the short-story form, Hemingway's short stories are an integral and important part of his achievement.

SARAH ORNE JEWETT (1849–1909). Sarah Orne Jewett was born in South Berwick, Maine, and lived there all her life, except for frequent visits in Boston, New York, and Philadelphia, a trip to the West, and an extended tour in Europe. No training could have been more important to the future observer and sympathetic recorder of New England village and seacoast life than the lessons in kindness and understanding given by her father, a country doctor, to the little girl who loved to accompany him on his rounds. In December, 1869, *The Atlantic Monthly* published "Mr. Bruce," the first of the long list of her stories to appear in its pages in the next few decades; her first book, *Deephaven*, appeared in 1877. Miss Jewett's work was firmly and serenely grounded in New England and drew its strength from her understanding of humble New England lives, but it was in no sense parochial. To read *The Letters of Sarah Orne Jewett*, edited by her lifelong friend Annie Fields (Boston, 1911), or F. O. Matthiessen's critical and biographical study, *Sarah Orne Jewett* (1929), is to realize that she wrote in perfect awareness of the central traditions and significant contemporary developments in American, English, and Continental fiction.

JAMES JOYCE (1882–1941). Born in Dublin, Joyce was trained for the priesthood, but broke away from the faith after struggling with his conscience much as Stephen Dedalus, the hero of his autobiographical first novel (*A Portrait of the Artist as a Young Man*, 1916), struggled with his. He left Ireland for the Continent, living at various times in Rome, Trieste, and Zurich, sometimes supporting himself by teaching languages; he finally settled in Paris and devoted himself exclusively to writing.

The commanding position which Joyce occupied in the world of letters between the two wars was first and foremost a result of the aims he realized, and the startling, varied techniques by which he realized them, in his two most ambitious novels, *Ulysses* (Paris, 1922) and *Finnegans Wake* (1939). But these brilliant performances should not make us forget his earliest work of fiction, *Dubliners*, a collection of short stories ready for publication in 1907 which, because of difficulties with political censorship both in Dublin and in London, was not published until 1914. Each of these stories — Joyce originally thought of calling them "Epiphanies" — reveals the life of a citizen of Dublin, with the utmost economy and rightness of form. They may be compared with the stories of Chekhov more appropriately than with any other stories, but in the end they are incomparable; there is a mood, experienced by the reader who has once come under the spell of their cool, precise beauty, when they seem, quite simply, to be the most perfect stories in English.

D. H. LAWRENCE (1885–1930). Lawrence was born in the Midlands mining district of England, the son of a miner; the circumstances of his early life must fairly have resembled those of the miners' families depicted in many of his works — in *Sons and Lovers* (1913), for instance. He started life as a school teacher, but here he felt cramped and stifled, and the publication of his early poems, stories, and novels made it clear that another vocation awaited him that would make it possible to seek the milder climates necessary to his frail health. His first novel, *The White Peacock* (1911), was followed quickly by many others; his most widely discussed novel, *Lady Chatterley's Lover*, was published in 1928. His first volume of short stories, *The Prussian Officer and Other Stories*, appeared in 1914. He traveled widely, in Germany, Italy, Mexico, the United States, and Australia, and lived much of his later life in Italy. He died in Vence, in the south of France. He wrote many books of travel and literary criticism, among them *Twilight in Italy* (1921), *Studies in Classic American Literature* (1923 — a most exciting and unconventional book in spite of its conventional title), and *Mornings in Mexico* (1927). There are numerous biographies, but the best source of insight into his life and opinions is still *The Letters of D. H. Lawrence*, edited with an introduction by Aldous Huxley.

ALUN LEWIS (1915–1944). To many who know this young Welsh writer's poems and stories, it seems altogether likely that his death by accident while on active duty in Burma was the heaviest loss sustained by British letters during the recent war.

His published work consists of four volumes: two volumes of poetry, *Raiders' Dawn* (1942) and *Ha! Ha! among the Trumpets* (1945); a volume of short stories, *The Last Inspection* (1942); and a volume jointly composed of further short stories and a selection of letters written during the war to his parents and his wife, *In the Green Tree* (1949). Everything he wrote, whether in prose or verse, is marked by a sanity, an integrity, a clarity and power of imaginative vision, an unassuming, simple dignity which are beyond praise. *In the Green Tree* contains a brief critical preface by A. L. Rowse and a postscript-memoir by Gwyn Jones. A fine, movingly sympathetic glimpse of him is provided by J. Maclaren-Ross in "Second Lieutenant Lewis," published in *Penguin New Writing*, No. 27 (April, 1946).

MAUPASSANT, HENRI-RENÉ-ALBERT-GUY DE (1850–1893). Maupassant, whose novels and tales fill twenty-odd volumes in the standard French edition of his works, is known to even the most casual reader of the short story through such classic examples of the "arranged" story as "The Necklace" and "A Piece of String." It may perhaps be taken for granted that he has been one of the two most important nineteenth-century models (Chekhov is the other) for later practice of the short-story form. Perhaps his best-known works, besides such stories as those mentioned above, are *Boule de Suif* (1880) and *Mademoiselle Fifi* (1883) for the *nouvelle*, and *Une Vie* (1883), *Bel Ami* (1885), and *Fort comme la Mort* (1889) for the novel. It is to be hoped that the tendency to patronize Maupassant, even on the part of those who recognize his evident stature and the scope of his work, will be remedied by Mr. Francis Steegmuller's admirable critical biography, *Maupassant: A Lion in the Path* (1949). In this book Mr. Steegmuller makes it clear that Maupassant is considerable not merely because of the bulk of his work, or as the perpetrator of moderately interesting fictional *feux d'artifice*, but as a writer of great and fundamental power and insight, possessing a mastery of technique which made Henry James describe him, in the phrase quoted in Mr. Steegmuller's title, as "a lion in the path."

WILLIAM SANSOM (1912–   ). During the past few years William Sansom has become increasingly well known, in America as well as in his native England, as a short-story writer who can be depended on to exploit subject-matter which it seems never to have occurred to anyone else to treat. Some of his subjects were offered him by his services as a fire-fighter in London during the war; he has contributed a brief record of that arduous life, "A

Fireman's Journal," to the collection of war-time diaries edited by Stefan Schimanski and Henry Treece, *Leaves in the Storm*. In his work the humblest and most banal features and episodes of daily life, scrutinized from new angles of vision and rendered in brushwork of an amazing richness and finesse, give up secrets and reveal powers which they would never have been suspected of possessing. His principal work thus far consists of four volumes of short stories (see the Reading List, below) and a novel, *The Body* (1949).

DYLAN THOMAS (1914–). Although Dylan Thomas is best known as a poet (*18 Poems*, 1934; *25 Poems*, 1936; *Deaths and Entrances*, 1946), his poems can scarcely have given more immediate or lasting pleasure than that afforded by the stories which make up *A Portrait of the Artist as a Young Dog* (1940). These stories of Welsh life and character as seen through the sharp, frank, unflinching eyes of childhood and boyhood are as warm-hearted, as imaginative, and very often as funny as any stories in English. Other prose, of a different order, is included along with verse in *The Map of Love* (1939).

EUDORA WELTY (1909–). Miss Welty is the daughter of an insurance salesman, and a native of Jackson, Mississippi, where, it has been said, she lives without any of the fuss and indulgence which many lesser authoresses allow themselves. She has attended the Columbia School of Journalism, and has twice won the O. Henry Memorial Prize for best short story of the year. In addition to three volumes of short stories she has written two novels, *The Robber Bridegroom* (1942) and *Delta Wedding* (1946).

Since the purpose of this list is simply to guide the beginning reader through the card catalogue of a library, details of place and date of publication are not given.

SHERWOOD ANDERSON: *Winesburg, Ohio*

ELIZABETH BOWEN: *Ivy Gripped the Steps*

KAY BOYLE: *The White Horses of Vienna; Thirty Stories*

ANTON CHEKHOV: *Select Tales; The Schoolmistress and Other Stories; The Chorus Girl and Other Stories*, etc. (All translated by Constance Garnett.)

JOHN COLLIER: *Presenting Moonshine*

ALEX COMFORT: *Letters from an Outpost*

JOSEPH CONRAD: *'Twixt Land and Sea; Youth and Two Other Stories; A Set of Six; Tales of Unrest*

STEPHEN CRANE: *Twenty Stories*

WILLIAM FAULKNER: *These Thirteen; Doctor Martino and Other Stories*

F. SCOTT FITZGERALD: *The Viking Portable Library F. Scott Fitzgerald*

E. M. FORSTER: *The Eternal Moment; The Celestial Omnibus*

NIKOLAI GOGOL: *The Overcoat*

GRAHAM GREENE: *Nineteen Stories*

THOMAS HARDY: *Wessex Tales; Life's Little Ironies*

BRET HARTE: *The Luck of Roaring Camp and Other Stories*

ERNEST HEMINGWAY: *Short Stories:* the First Forty-Nine Stories and the Play *The Fifth Column*

ALDOUS HUXLEY: *Brief Candles; Young Archimedes; Mortal Coils*

HENRY JAMES: *Short Stories*, selected by Clifton Fadiman

SARAH ORNE JEWETT: *A White Heron; The Country of the Pointed Firs*

JAMES JOYCE: *Dubliners*

RUDYARD KIPLING: *Plain Tales from the Hills*

RING LARDNER: *Round Up*

D. H. LAWRENCE: *The Prussian Officer; Collected Tales*

ALUN LEWIS: *The Last Inspection; In the Green Tree*

J. MACLAREN-ROSS: *The Stuff to Give the Troops*

THOMAS MANN: *Stories of Three Decades*

KATHERINE MANSFIELD: *The Garden Party; The Dove's Nest; Bliss*

W. SOMERSET MAUGHAM: *Ah King; Tales of East and West; The Mixture as Before*

GUY DE MAUPASSANT: *Boule de Suif and Other Stories: a New Translation* by H. N. P. Sloman

JOHN O'HARA: *The Doctor's Son; Files on Parade*

WILLIAM PLOMER: *Paper Houses; Four Countries*

KATHERINE ANNE PORTER: *Pale Horse, Pale Rider; The Leaning Tower*

V. S. PRITCHETT: *It May Never Happen*

WILLIAM SANSOM: *Three; Fireman Flower; South; Something Terrible, Something Lovely*

WILLIAM SAROYAN: *The Daring Young Man on the Flying Trapeze; Little Children; The Trouble with Tigers*

JOHN STEINBECK: *The Long Valley*

PETER TAYLOR: *A Long Fourth*

DYLAN THOMAS: *A Portrait of the Artist as a Young Dog*

IVAN TURGENEV: *A Sportsman's Sketches*

EVELYN WAUGH: *Mr. Loveday's Little Outing; Work Suspended*

EUDORA WELTY: *A Curtain of Green; The Wide Net; The Golden Apples*

THOMAS WOLFE: *From Death to Morning*